TORQUEMADA

By Howard Fast

TORQUEMADA

AGRIPPA'S DAUGHTER

THE HILL

POWER

APRIL MORNING

THE HOWARD FAST READER

THE WINSTON AFFAIR

MOSES, PRINCE OF EGYPT

SILAS TIMBERMAN

THE PASSION OF SACCO AND
  VANZETTI

SPARTACUS

THE PROUD AND THE FREE

MY GLORIOUS BROTHERS

CLARKTON

THE AMERICAN

FREEDOM ROAD

CITIZEN TOM PAINE

THE UNVANQUISHED

THE LAST FRONTIER

CONCEIVED IN LIBERTY

PLACE IN THE CITY

THE CHILDREN

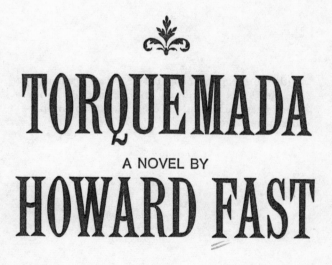

TORQUEMADA

A NOVEL BY

HOWARD FAST

1966

DOUBLEDAY & COMPANY, INC., GARDEN CITY, NEW YORK

With the exception of actual historical personages,
the characters are entirely the product of the au-
thor's imagination and have no relation to any per-
sons in real life.

FOR

JEROME

AND

JULIUS

AND

RENA

CHAPTER ONE

IN THE YEAR 1483 a tall, lean man in the black habit of a Dominican friar walked along a street in Segovia. His name was Thomas de Torquemada, and there were few people in Segovia who did not know him by sight. He had the reputation of being a righteous man and his reputation as such went far beyond the limits of Segovia.

It was late afternoon, and the sunlight was still hard and bright. The shadows had hard edges and the light itself was hard and brittle. On this particular street there was an unbroken stretch of white, windowless walls, and though he had seen these walls a thousand times before, the sight of them now pricked at Torquemada's fancy and made him wonder whether a street in the Holy City might not have walls as white and gleaming.

On this street there was no one at all. But on the next street that Torquemada came to, a group of half-naked children played in the dust. When they looked up and saw Torquemada, they crossed themselves and fled. This evidence of fear on their part touched him and hurt him more than most people would imagine, and though his high-boned face did not change, he winced inwardly. There were times when Thomas de Torquemada attempted to understand or to explain to himself the manner in which he was held and regarded by the people in the town. He was never wholly successful in this and, of late, he practiced it less frequently.

Torquemada came to the central square of Segovia and walked across it. It was the end of the siesta time and the only one there was a drunken, red-nosed old watchman who had taken his siesta in the dirt by the fountain and who now sat up and greeted Torquemada with an open, yawning mouth and an ugly whiskered face. In Torquemada's sight, the face of this man crawled with ugliness and with the memory of sin. Sometimes it seemed to Torquemada that he could look at a man's face and see sin as a splash of purple paint. Now, in the hot sunlight, the streets and the walls of the town rippled and moved and came alive in answer to Torquemada's sudden, fierce thought of sin. He stifled this thought, knowing that if he allowed it to enlarge itself and to dominate him, it would spoil his entire afternoon. He had no desire to have his afternoon spoiled.

He came soon to the eastern boundaries of Segovia, where the mansions of the rich and the powerful families stood. These great homes, one after another, sat within their own garden walls. There were

seven of them in a row and the third from the edge
of the town was the house of Alvero de Rafel.

As Torquemada came to the gate in the wall that
surrounded the home of the Rafels, he paused and
breathed the smell of their rose garden and let his
irritation quiet itself and disappear. He was particularly sensitive this afternoon to impressions, to
sounds, smells, motions and even to the waves in the
air set up by the heat; and now the sight and smell
of a rose garden and of a dark and beautiful girl
kneeling in this rose garden blessed him, he felt, as
a benediction. The sight covered him with vanity
and gave him pride in the manner of his existence.
He knew that this was a sinful feeling and he bore
it with guilt; but nevertheless he felt renewed and
he smiled at the girl as she rose and saw him and
greeted him.

In the meanwhile Julio, the old footman of the
Rafels, had come to open the gate. Torquemada
thanked him politely for this but, like so many of
the simple people in Segovia, Julio avoided his
glance. Not so with Catherine de Rafel, who ran to
him and embraced him, and said to him,

"I welcome you, dear Father."

Torquemada held the girl next to him in response
to a need—a very great need. He felt her warm and
pliable form against him, and he promised himself
that he would do penance for that. He would go to
confession and he would light candles, but meanwhile he felt enlarged and gratified. He looked down
upon Catherine from his tall, lean height and
touched her hair. That was his privilege. He had

13

known this dark, beautiful girl since the day of her birth. She was now twenty-two years old. He was as much her father as her real father in blood, and there was no reason why he should not embrace her and touch her hair and even lay a finger upon her cheek—knowing that each action was an action of innocence. He had to articulate this and he replied,

"To me you are purity and goodness in the flesh. I don't suppose I could make you understand how often I hunger for that. Goodness is the food that my soul wants but one does not find it in large supply in Segovia, so I look at you with great joy, dear Catherine."

"Good Father." Catherine smiled. "You know women so little. No, you mustn't take offense," she added, watching his face change. "I mean that there is one part of a woman you don't know. A woman's soul you know three hundred times better than I would ever know it. I make no sense, do I? I am glad to see you. Take the roses I cut."

She gave him her basket of fresh-cut roses and asked whether they should go inside. Torquemada studied her for a long moment and then nodded, a slight smile playing across his face and giving him an unusual charm. Catherine often noticed how pleasant it could be when hard-faced and morose people smiled. If you respected such people their smile was a gift and it had great power.

Now she took Torquemada's arm and led him into the house. They entered the gallery which was connected with the garden by a Moorish archway. All of the houses in Segovia at that time had a Moorish

14

influence, but the Rafel house was large and old and had been built entirely by the Moors. The floors were of blue tile, and the walls of fine African plaster. The gallery was a great room some forty feet long and twenty feet wide. One whole side of this room consisted of Moorish archways and lovely sustaining columns that twisted sinuously and beautifully. Through these columns one saw the pretty prospect of the rose garden. Maria de Rafel, Catherine's mother, had drapes made for the entire length of this side of the room. When the drapes were closed, the room became a contained place in itself—but when the drapes were drawn back, as they were now, room and garden blended together, the big-leafed African ivy invading the house from the garden and twining itself around the columns. Within the long gallery, the furnishings were simple enough. There was a fireplace in the very middle of the wall and around it were six big armchairs. At the far end of the room, when one entered from the garden, there was a long refectory table and around it were eight tall, straight-backed chairs. On the floor there was a golden rug from Morocco and on the wall portraits of Alvero de Rafel, of Maria, his wife, and of Lomas, his wife's father—all of them painted by the artist Consaloes.

Maria, Catherine's mother, was alone in the room when Catherine and Torquemada entered; and she looked up with pleasure, laid aside the embroidery she was working on and rose. Maria was forty-two years old and still beautiful, shapely and desirable, and she smiled easily to make Torquemada welcome. Thus it was always at the house of Rafel. He felt welcome, he felt wanted, he felt cherished. The fact that a man is a priest does not kill his desire to be cherished, and Torquemada had that sense of his own courtliness, his own dignity—so indispensable to a Spanish gentleman—as he walked toward Maria de Rafel with his hands held out.

"My dear Señora Maria," he said.

Then he took her hands and bowed and kissed her right hand and then her left hand. There was no gentleman in Segovia who could have done it with more grace and ease, a fact that mother and daughter noticed and appreciated.

Maria, who was a rather precise person, resumed her seat, took up her embroidery again and, working with concentration and precision on the tiny stitches, said to Torquemada, "I dreamed of an avenging angel last night. Now listen, good Prior. He stood in front of me, so proud and angry that I thought my heart would break with fear. Oh, where is the shield of my Lord God and Christ, His Son? I mean this is exactly what I asked myself in the dream, and a moment later, the good Thomas stood between us. He sheltered me and here you are in the flesh. Do you know that eleven days have gone by since we saw you last? However, my dream told me that you would be here today."

Catherine sat down in the chair next to her mother but Torquemada remained standing and expressed his thanks and his appreciation. "However," he said, "I am not sure that this reliance on dreams is entirely Christian, yet today I shall not question it. I

16

am overcome by warmth. Since I have been appointed Inquisitor I find little enough warmth from those I knew."

"Because they don't know you as we do," Catherine said.

"You are both of you comforting women and this house is a light, a warm haven. Why did I allow eleven days to go by? This is penance. If I punish others, I must punish myself even more."

"I will not listen to talk of punishment," Maria interrupted, "certainly not here. You know, Father Thomas, that if you praise our house you must bring charity to it, only charity, and charity and punishment are not exactly the same thing—won't you agree, Father Thomas?"

"I agree and I beg your forgiveness."

"And so," Maria continued, "you will stay and dine with us."

Torquemada shook his head. "Ah—I am afraid not, I must leave for Seville tonight. By the King's command. This however is not a statement of pride. I have no love for Seville."

"But you see," Maria said excitedly, "fate or coincidence is very much with us, and unlike you, good Father, I believe that a dream can be a very Christian thing indeed. Now consider. Alvero also leaves for Seville tonight. You leave by the King's command, he leaves by the Queen's command."

"Then we can travel together." Torquemada nodded. "The roads are dangerous these days, more dangerous than you would believe, madam, but with

17

Alvero riding at my right hand what should I fear, whom should I fear?"

"Whom indeed," Catherine said, "and since Juan rides with him, there is more than safety— How do I dare to talk this way?" She blushed and bowed her head to cover her confusion, and her mother said to Torquemada,

"She is very much in love, Father Thomas."

"So I felt, so I sensed. Love is a holy thing, a holy thing that fills this good house—"

His curious, almost violent declamation in praise of love was interrupted by the shouts of stable boys and the clatter of horses' hooves. Catherine rose expectantly and a moment later her father and her betrothed lover came into the room. Her father, Alvero de Rafel was a tall, good-looking man of about forty-seven—his broad face and wide-set eyes giving him an appearance of forthrightness and inspiring confidence in the beholder. His eyes were dark blue under his straight brows and, unlike so many of the Spanish dons of his time, he was beardless. A little behind him, Catherine's lover—Juan Pomas, a handsome, thin-faced, young man of twenty-three. Like Alvero, Pomas was dressed for the road, booted, spurred, cloaked and wearing sword and dagger. The two of them made a gallant and impressive sight as they strode into the room. Catherine ran to them—to be embraced by her father and to have her hand kissed by Pomas, who was immediately uneasy in the presence of Torquemada.

However, for Alvero, there were no barriers and after he had kissed his daughter he took the Prior's hand with warmth and eagerness. They were old friends and they shared the voiceless communication that old, close friends can engage in. While they exchanged their greetings Maria came to her husband and kissed him gently and evenly upon the cheek, making Torquemada wonder how much there was left between these two, who had come to this formal and precise relationship out of all the fierce fires of their youth. That youth was not so far away that Torquemada could not recall it exactly and totally. Such memories were only yesterday for him and sometimes he wondered whether perhaps he was exempt from the normal passage of time. He came to himself to hear them talking about the journey and to listen to Alvero's pleasure in the fact that he, the Prior, would be with them. Old Julio brought wine. There was a special, heavy and sweet wine that agreed with Torquemada's taste. Alvero poured it into goblets and said to him,

"God speed our journey. You will drink with us, Father Thomas?"

"I drink with you and I ride with you. If you will have me."

Alvero handed a glass of wine to his wife and said to her,

"If we will have him, now listen to that, Maria. If we will have him."

He turned back to Torquemada. "Thomas, old friend, let me tell you this, we will have you. You will deal with the Devil and we will deal with the thieves."

"Put less faith in my competence," Torquemada

19

said. "I trust you with thieves. Don't trust me with the Devil. Have doubts about me, Alvero."

"Impossible. I have no doubts. Look at them."

He nodded to where Juan and Catherine were walking toward the farther end of the room.

"Why are they so impatient? They have time enough."

"But better use for it than we have, my husband," Maria said.

"I suppose so." Alvero nodded; and suddenly Torquemada had the feeling that the warmth in his host's mouth and in his heart had become cold and tasteless. Alvero struggled loose from this momentary depression. He raised his glass and gave them their health,

"*Salut!* Good family and good friends."

The others drank with him. Alvero stared at his glass, then suddenly he turned and hurled it into the hearth where it shattered. Torquemada watched him curiously.

Himself now, Alvero said quietly,

"I ask for no greater happiness. That glass is sacred. No one else drinks from it. That's a small passage of wisdom, don't you agree with me, Thomas?"

"I agree," Torquemada replied, watching Alvero thoughtfully.

CHAPTER TWO

To REACH THE HIGH ROAD that ran south from Segovia to Seville, one went from the house of Alvero through the town and up onto what was then known as the Jews' Ridge. It was late twilight when Alvero and Juan Pomas and the peon Julio came through Segovia toward the high road. The two dons were mounted on fine Arab steeds—Alvero on a pure white thoroughbred, and Juan on a black horse, an Arab filly, slight, nervous and strong. Trailing behind them, Julio rode a clumsy cob and led a pack mule. Cobs were called British horses because, long ago, some of the original stock had come from that faraway island.

Alvero led them through the town at a walk, so that the small children already asleep would not be awakened and so that their mothers would not send the travelers on their journey with curses. At the far side of the town, a young man lounged against a gateway and serenaded a maiden who was unseen in the darkness. Alvero stopped his horse to listen and Juan and Julio closed up behind him. In a clear, tenor voice the young man sang,

> *"And when I journey far away,*
> *Who will care for my true love?*
> *Night will lighten into day—*
> *Who will care for my true love."*

"A Castilian song," said Alvero. "When I was young, all the young men in Spain sang Castilian songs. What do they sing today, Juan?"

"They sing very little indeed," Juan answered dully. His spirits were low. He felt no exaltation about a trip to Seville in the company of Prior Thomas de Torquemada, and yet he lacked the courage to withdraw. He was somewhat afraid of Alvero but he was much more afraid of Torquemada, and this fear was something that Alvero could understand. It often occurred to Alvero that in the strange land that Spain had become, one of the strangest things was his own friendship for the Inquisitor, Thomas de Torquemada. But friendship transcends fear. This was axiomatic, he thought to himself. He was a Spanish knight, and he had small patience with fear. Deep inside him he suspected that Juan Pomas was a coward, but this was something which he suspected and which he had not dealt with. Even in his thoughts he refrained from dealing with it —because he sensed a complexity that went beyond the simple premises of knighthood. Alvero recognized such complexities as the increment of age. The older he became, the less simple were the answers to problems, and the problems themselves were increasingly complex.

They had left the city behind now and, as they mounted the dirt track to the high road, Alvero saw Torquemada sitting on his horse at the lip of the hill and waiting for them. There he sat on his big horse, grimly and stiffly, wearing his monkish habit, the pearl-gray luminescent sky of twilight making a backdrop for him, and the last rays of the sun behind him. He was a firm and angry servant of God, and for some reason it pleased Alvero to see him cast in this light—while the somber mood of the darkening twilight covered Alvero like a comfortable cloak and soothed his Spanish soul.

They all sat their horses together for a moment on the high road, looking back at Segovia beneath them—at the old Roman aqueduct looming over the city, disappearing into a hole of night; and then, in the city, like a single candle, a finger of light came into being. Alvero looked at Torquemada, who nodded.

"An act of faith," Torquemada said. "A woman is being burned at the stake. I thought of it when I walked through the streets of Segovia this morning. They looked at me and they said, there is Torquemada who burns men and women at the stake. God help me if I burn their bodies. Their souls live naked and clean."

"I would lie to you," Alvero said, "if I did not tell

you that I take no joy in the sight of what you call an act of faith."

"Do I find joy in it, Alvero? And tell me, my friend, what do you call it if not an act of faith?"

Alvero shook his head and spurred his horse up to the road. Juan and Julio followed him and then, behind them, Torquemada.

An hour later they stopped at an inn. The landlord, a man whom Alvero had known for years, recognized Torquemada and out of this recognition the innkeeper became taciturn and withdrawn. They ate in the common dining room of the inn, but whispers walled them off from the other men who were present there. Alvero realized that it was the first time he had been together on a journey of any kind with Torquemada since the Prior had become an Inquisitor. He felt a curious pity for the priest—who ate sparingly and remained silent.

The following day was cool and sunny, with blue skies and a soothing wind. Alvero's spirits revived and, together with Juan, he sang a song to his horse as they went. Torquemada listened and smiled. They stopped to eat at the roadside and made a meal of wine and sausage that they had brought with them from the inn. Then they continued along the road.

Half of the life of Spain flowed along that road from Seville to Segovia. They met merchants with long trains of pack horses and with armed guards, five men in light armor to guard each pack horse. They met monks and priests and friars and once a bishop, riding in great majesty with over thirty attendants gathered around him on horses and don-

keys and mules. They passed tumblers and jugglers
—and once a party of two hundred of the King's men
who were riding to hold a part of the border against
the Moors.

They all fell into the pace of the journey. They
became easier with each other and easier with their
words and, bit by bit, the hard mask of Torquemada
softened. He sat with them when they roasted their
food over a fire at the roadside. He stretched his legs
in the inns and listened to the talk and to the stories,
and the farther they got from Segovia, the fewer
were the people who recognized him. He and Alvero talked a great deal about the old days and Juan
listened to them respectfully.

And then one day they topped a rise in the road
and saw before them the walls of Seville.

The following day Alvero and Juan dressed themselves in their best clothes and walked through Seville to the palace of Ferdinand and Isabella. In hose
and doublet, wearing light half-armor of polished
steel, chased with gold, the two men made a handsome sight. They were fine-looking, Spanish gentlemen and when they came to the palace, they were
recognized and greeted warmly by Don Louis Al-
vadan, who was Queen Isabella's private secretary.
He had been waiting for them and watching for
them so that they would not lose themselves in the
bustle and turmoil of the Court. Juan had never
been to the King's Court before and he watched the
press of knights and ladies and diplomats and merchants and dukes and counts with excitement and
delight.

As Don Louis led them toward Isabella's chambers, he explained to Alvero that their arrival was particularly fortuitous. "The Queen," Don Louis said, "had been discussing a matter of some importance with a Genoese sailor by the name of Christopher Columbus." Columbus had a notion of opening up some new and possibly very profitable trade routes for Spain. There were those who supported his ideas and those who thought him entirely mad. They entered Isabella's chamber now and Don Louis dropped his voice and then cut short his explanation. He stood just inside the doorway, waiting, Alvero and Juan beside him.

Alvero looked about the room and at his Queen with curiosity. The palace itself had been so recently conquered by the Spaniards that they were hardly settled there—almost like people at an inn. Isabella's chamber had high-arched ceilings in the Moorish style, Moorish pillars and archways. The stone walls were draped with the banners and rugs of the House of Castile, and a wooden platform had been built so that the Queen might have a chair above the level of the floor. On this platform there were two chairs and a table—and the Queen herself was bent over the table, staring at maps. The man called Columbus stood next to her. In his late thirties, Columbus was tall, almost cadaverously lean, with deep hollows in his face that gave him a curiously esthetic look. He could not restrain or conceal his passion, even in front of the Queen.

It was two years since Alvero had seen the Queen. She was thirty-four now, a strange, reserved, imperious and almost sexless woman, who could nevertheless be curiously tender and very charming. Alvero knew that she had noted their entrance. Nevertheless, she did not raise her eyes; and her imperious voice, nagging and petulant, filled the chamber.

"Why, why, why, Signor Columbus? You are becoming my own personal devil. You plead with me until your voice troubles my dreams. Why, why do I need an empire? Spain is large enough and never forget that part of this Holy Land is still held by the Moors."

"My Lady, I abase myself," Columbus answered. "I despise myself because I must disagree with you. Still I must say to you, my Queen, can you imprison a man's dreams?"

"Do I stop you from dreaming?"

"The dreaming is nothing, your Highness, the doing is all. You are the Queen of a great country. I offer you a world. I offer you an empire and you will be an Empress."

"I have discussed this matter with my learned men, so many learned men, you know that."

"The learned men!" Columbus cried. "God above us, what do the learned men know? Have you discussed it with sailors, with fishermen? My noble Lady, I abase myself—still I must say to you that sailors have known for centuries that the world is round. This is not a new idea. Have you ever heard of the expression—hull down on the horizon—a ship with sails showing but body hidden by the curvature of the earth? Have you never heard of that expression? I abase myself before you. You are the Queen of Spain. I am nothing. Nevertheless—"

Isabella looked up deliberately and decided to notice Alvero. She clapped her hands with pleasure. "Alvero—my dear, good friend! To come so far and so quickly for a woman who doesn't know her own mind! Alvero, come and rescue me. This man is destroying me. This man is Columbus. He is a madman. Come to me, Alvero."

Alvero strode to the platform but stopped short of it and kneeled on the floor. He genuflected with real humility. This was a game he played with Isabella, yet he did not object to it. There was a strange relationship between the two of them. Isabella came to him and drew him to his feet. She instructed him to kiss her hand and he did so dutifully, and then, in a whisper in his ear, she asked him about Juan.

"Who is he, my dear Alvero? He is good-looking but he seems to have no character."

"My daughter's fiancé."

"Well, I think your daughter could do better. Is she a pretty girl?"

"Very beautiful, your Highness."

"Then she could certainly do better. Anyway, bring him here to me." The Queen pointed to Juan and crooked her finger. "Come here to me, young man. No, don't stand there like a fool, come here to me. Come over here and kneel down in front of me, the way your father-in-law did," and then to Alvero, "I am afraid he is a fool, Alvero."

Juan came to the Queen and knelt down at the

edge of the platform as he had seen Alvero do; but
the Queen decided that she had lost interest in him
and she took Alvero's hand and led him up onto the
platform and introduced him to Columbus. Alvero
was pleased to see that if Christopher Columbus of
Genoa was mad, he at least had a sense of humor.
His mouth twitched and he shook hands firmly with
Alvero. They liked each other. They both of them
felt that. Isabella began to whine, explaining once
again to Alvero that this was Signor Christopher
Columbus of Genoa in Italy and that he plagued
her. He had driven her to a point where she could
not exist with him and she could not exist without
him.

"He is willing to become a good Spaniard," she
cried petulantly, "but he cannot swear his allegiance
to a Queen, no, no, no, Alvero, he must make us an
Empress and find us a mighty empire in the Indies."

"I know of no woman more suited to be an Empress," Alvero began.

"I would have you whipped, you stupid man,"
Isabella cried. "You think to flatter me? Every
primping, strutting male in Spain practices the flat-
tery of his Queen. Only it doesn't become you, Don
Alvero. Talk sense. You are a merchant—I think the
most intelligent merchant in Spain. That's why I sent
for you. He wants a fleet of ships. Where shall we
find ships or the money to buy them?"

"Ships, my Lady? The way to the Indies by ship
is closed."

"Eastward, yes," Columbus said, "but, Señor Alvero, I propose to sail westward around the earth."

31

Both Columbus and the Queen watched Alvero's reaction. He was staring at Columbus, less surprised than intrigued by the man's notion. It was hardly a new notion. As Columbus said, a good many people, as a practical matter, knew that the world was round. Isabella now explained that it was his obsession. "The earth is a ball," she said. "He insists on that. So I sent for the wisest man in Spain."

"Do you agree with me, Don Alvero?" Columbus asked.

"Tell us, Alvero," the Queen prodded him. "Do they stand on their heads in the Indies?"

"On their heads, no, my Lady," Alvero answered slowly. "Yet the earth is a ball. Travelers have known that for many years—"

Don Louis had re-entered the chamber while they were talking. He moved about obsequiously, here and there, from one side of the platform to the other, until Isabella burst out in annoyance,

"I told you we were not to be disturbed, Don Louis."

"The King is impatient."

"Then let him remain impatient. He can wait, his inquisition can wait and this Torquemada can wait. I have no desire to see this man Torquemada."

"You promised his Majesty, my Lady."

"Oh, I will punish you, make sure of that," Isabella cried. "You stupid man. I will have you whipped, drawn and quartered!" and then to Alvero, "No, don't look at me like that. I don't mean a word of it. He's stupid." Then she sighed and said to Don Louis, "Very well, bring them here."

Don Louis left the room and Isabella demanded
to know what kind of a man this Torquemada was.
Her manner fascinated Alvero. She had changed so
since he had last seen her. Imperious, whining, petulant, pleading, her mood and manner shifted in-
credibly from moment to moment. Alvero wondered
how anyone could live with this woman or be with
her—and yet the entire Court revolved more around
her than around her husband. He began to tell her of
Torquemada, and then suddenly she interrupted
him to dismiss Columbus. She dismissed him with a
wave of her hand. "Get out of our sight, Italian,"
she said to him. "We have had enough of you. Now
leave us!"

Juan was still kneeling as Columbus backed out of
the room and Isabella looked at him with disbelief.

"Get up off your knees, you stupid man," she said.
Juan rose to his feet. Isabella turned to Alvero and
said that she supposed Juan would have stayed
there, kneeling on the floor all afternoon if no one
had told him different. "Was it that way when we
were young, Alvero? I mean the young men that
were you and your friends? No, don't bother answer-
ing. We were talking about Torquemada. What manner of man is he?"

"I have known him all my life," Alvero said.

"He is a friend?"

"Yes, he is a friend." Alvero nodded.

"Then how can you judge him?" the Queen
asked. "Do you know my husband is going to make
him Chief Inquisitor? Yes, exactly, the head of the
Inquisition all over Spain."

33

"God help him," Alvero whispered in spite of himself. It was at that moment that Ferdinand, the King, came into the room, Torquemada walking behind him.

Ferdinand was a skinny, nervous man, slight, smaller than his wife and increasingly a victim of an incurable illness. He had a hacking cough and he was as alert and as sensitive as a bird. He feared people and he was jealous of his wife. He saw Alvero standing beside her and he was jealous. He saw Juan, a younger man, and he was jealous. His jealousy was anxious and free-floating. He feared, he envied, he hated. He hopped up to the wooden platform and examined the maps and then cried out aloud that the world was not round. He knew Alvero but had not the courtesy to greet him; but, instead, went into a harangue about the shape of the earth. He hated Columbus. He expectorated superstitiously and crossed himself and then went into a long, disjointed explanation to Torquemada concerning Columbus and what Columbus believed and what Columbus desired. Like his wife, Isabella, he fell easily into a pattern of whimpering, and now he complained to Torquemada,

"Heresy, Prior, heresy, heresy. Don't you agree? Yes, you must agree, of course."

"Sir, my husband," Isabella burst out. "You're acting like a pig. Do you hear me? Like a pig! Here's Alvero de Rafel and you have not so much as nodded to him. Where is our royal dignity, our reputation?"

Ferdinand expectorated on the map in front of her. He wiped his spittle with his fingers and then demanded again of Torquemada whether or not the mere statement that the world was round should not be considered as heresy.

Torquemada replied that it was certainly idiocy but that all idiocy could not be marked as heresy. Alvero had a feeling that, in front of him, Torquemada was pleading for approval—for friendship— perhaps even for hope. "He is already the Grand Inquisitor," Alvero said to himself. Torquemada was stiff, very much self-contained, and Alvero sensed his agony. "How he must suffer," Alvero said to himself.

Ferdinand clenched his fist and pounded on the table, on the map, and cried out, "He's a Jew!"

"Who, sire?" Torquemada asked.

"The Italian, Columbus."

"But a Christian now, from all that I hear," Torquemada said softly.

"But a Christian now!" Ferdinand burst out, "but a Christian now! Oh, I tell you, that's fine talk from a man I have just appointed Chief Inquisitor. Here is a Jew-Christian tied up in a big, fat knot and the Chief Inquisitor argues with me!"

His voice soft and legalistic, Torquemada said rapidly, "If he Judaizes, we can take action against him. But there must be some proof, legal proof. At the very least, we must have an accusation—"

"They all Judaize!" Ferdinand shouted, "including that one." He pointed at Don Alvero, and with great calm and without raising his voice, Torquemada said,

"He is no Jew, sire, not even a converted Jew."

"They are all Jews up there in Segovia!" Ferdinand shouted. "Every one of them with that bastard taint in his blood. Every one of them, every one of them—"

Isabella took Alvero's arm and led him off the platform. "Go out of here, my friend," she whispered to him. Alvero nodded at Juan. They paused at the doorway. Isabella began to cry, and Alvero could not help thinking how odd it was to see her in tears. Suddenly it brought to mind, very forcefully, the fact that she was a woman. The actual fact of it was that no one ever thought of a Queen as a woman. Juan said this after they had left the palace. "Suddenly she became a woman," he said to Alvero. And without replying, Alvero thought to himself, "God help her."

CHAPTER THREE

ON THEIR WAY BACK to Segovia, all three men and perhaps Julio, the peon, as well, were highly aware of what had taken place in Seville. Yet it was not until they were close to the outskirts of Segovia that the subject was mentioned, and even then it came about circuitously. They had been riding for some hours in silence, Torquemada and Alvero side by side at the front, and Juan and Julio a few hundred yards in the rear. Deep in his own thoughts, Alvero could not recall afterwards what had prompted him to mention to Torquemada that twenty years had passed since the priest had baptized his daughter.

"It seems like yesterday," Alvero said.

Torquemada spoke sententiously. He said that time is a moment. He said that a man's life is a moment. The sands ran through an hourglass. Suddenly, as if aware of the pretentious nonsense that he was

39

talking, he cut off his words. It was only in front of Rafel that he was ashamed of being a priest.

But as if he had not noticed at all, Alvero said, "And five years before that I came to Segovia and knew you for the first time, Thomas."

"Yes, I remember," Torquemada nodded. Suddenly he was full of his memories. "From where, Alvero? From where did you come?"

Alvero became wary. When a Spaniard is wary, he is part animal, and it seemed to Torquemada that Alvero crouched lower on his horse, shielded himself, touched his sword. It came as a surprise. The question on Torquemada's part had been neither innocent nor probing. It was a pointless question. His thoughts moved in one direction, his words in another. As of the moment before, he could not recall that he cared a tittle where Alvero had come from; and now Alvero was wary and afraid.

"Twenty-five years," Alvero said slowly. "You never asked me that before. Why, Thomas, why never before in twenty-five years?"

"Surely I asked you," Torquemada protested.

"Perhaps." Alvero nodded. He made a visible attempt to shed his wariness. He turned the conversation to Columbus and, in a fairly rational manner, they were able to discuss the question of whether or not the earth was round.

"Of course," Torquemada said, "you merchants know, don't you? You do know; I mean you have always known. I mean, in a way, it is a brotherhood."

"What is a brotherhood?" Alvero asked him.

"Of merchants."

"Of merchants?" Alvero repeated.

"I mean simply—well, for example, yourself and the man Columbus. You are both merchants. You share certain knowledge. You share a matter of maps. Isn't that so?"

"I don't quite know what you mean," Alvero said.

"Think about it."

Then they rode on in silence again.

It was late afternoon. They came to a stone road marker that was as old as time. On one side were the faint remains of an engraving in some lost script that was possibly Phoenician. On the other side was a Latin inscription that was still readable. The Latin inscription said, "four miles." That had often puzzled Alvero since they were only a mile and a half from the edge of Segovia. Here they rested their horses for a little while, Alvero and Torquemada sitting side by side, and Julio and Juan a respectable distance in the rear. Nodding at Juan, Torquemada said to Alvero,

"He keeps his distance, Alvero. Is he afraid of me?"

"I suppose so," Alvero replied.

"Why?"

"Do you ask? You are the Grand Inquisitor now, Thomas—over all of Spain."

"The Inquisition is God's arm," and when Alvero made no response to this, Torquemada said, "Do you fear me too, Alvero?"

"Thomas, we are old friends."

"Why did the Queen send for you, Alvero? You

say nothing about it. Is she going to back the Italian?"

"If we can find the money." Alvero nodded. "Shall we ride on now?"

Torquemada led the way. Alvero rode with his head down, puzzled and perturbed, lost in his own thoughts—thoughts that swept him into paths he refused to travel. It was almost with relief that he heard a cry for help. They were on the outskirts of the city now and spurring his horse ahead of the Prior, Alvero saw a struggling group of four men. A tight cluster, they pulled apart as Alvero's horse thundered down upon them. Three men had attacked a fourth. He stood with his arms covering his head. Even in the brief moment, Alvero noticed the long, black robe that he wore, and took it for granted that the man was a priest. It infuriated him that three cutthroats should leap on a priest in this manner. Suddenly Segovia was his city and the thieves had violated it. He drew his sword and roared at them, swept on to them, driving his horse directly at them and cut at them as he passed by. Behind him, Juan Pomas closed up the gap—as if relieved after so long with Torquemada to find something he did not fear and that he could strike out at. The three thieves ran, and Juan pursued them, cutting at them with his sword. Their screams of pain and their pleas for mercy came back to Alvero as he pulled in his horse and returned to the priest, and there dismounted.

Torquemada was already there, not dismounted but sitting on his horse, and looking darkly at the man they had rescued; and Alvero saw that the priest was not a priest but a rabbi, gray-bearded, and as different from a priest as one man could be from another. How had he mistaken him, Alvero asked himself and how had his mind leaped immediately to such a conclusion? Torquemada made no mistake. He and the rabbi faced each other. The rabbi, a man in his middle fifties, an impressive-looking man of medium height, had been hurt. A trickle of blood ran down the side of his head. His hat lay on the ground. Alvero dismounted and picked up the hat. He was highly conscious of Torquemada's piercing gaze as he returned the hat to the rabbi and asked the man whether he was hurt.

Dazed, the rabbi appeared to ponder the question and then he said, "I am a Jew."

Still breathing hard, still high and excited over the incident, Alvero said, "I didn't ask you that, I asked you whether you were hurt."

"Hurt?" The Jew appeared to ponder this before he replied that he was not hurt, just a single blow on the head. "No, I am all right."

Juan had returned now from his pursuit of the thieves and Julio had come up with the pack horse. Still mounted, Juan was watching Alvero curiously. Alvero told him to take the pack horse from Julio and instructed Julio to escort the Jew home. The rabbi shook his head.

"I don't need an escort, Don Alvero. The synagogue is only a stone's throw away."

Speaking suddenly and flatly, Torquemada said, "Jew, do I know you? Lift your face, man. You are a

43

rabbi, aren't you, from the looks of you? Lift your face so I can see it." Quite deliberately Mendoza took a few steps toward Torquemada and then looked up at him. "I think you know me, Prior Torquemada," he said.

"I see you, Rabbi Mendoza," Torquemada replied harshly. "I would not say that I know you, but I see you."

"As you will," Mendoza agreed with great calm and then he turned to Alvero and bowed slightly. "Thank you, Don Alvero de Rafel. I thank you and your man. I owe you my life." With that, he turned and walked off into the gathering darkness. Looking after him, Alvero shuddered—whether with fear or the increasing cold of night, he did not know. Yet he felt moved to say to Torquemada, "He knew my name. How do you suppose he knew my name? I never saw him before, Thomas." He was not being defensive, yet in spite of himself, he heard the note of fear and protest in his voice.

Torquemada replied that the cursed Jews knew everything. Directing a long finger after the rabbi, Torquemada said, "His name is Benjamin Mendoza. He is rabbi at the synagogue, and the devil's handyman. Better if you had let him die, Alvero."

Alvero glanced at Juan, who through all of this had said nothing, had only sat his horse and said nothing.

Then they went on. They stopped at the priory and took their leave of Torquemada, and a little while later Alvero was home.

All through dinner that evening Catherine de

Rafel watched Juan. His silence puzzled and confused her and she wondered whether he had had some kind of falling out with her father, but when she put this to him after dinner, he assured her that it was not the case. He formally requested permission from Alvero to take Catherine into the garden and Alvero, assenting, was relieved to have them gone. He could think of nothing but the encounter with the rabbi, and he had also studiously refrained from any mention of it at dinner. Neither had Juan mentioned it. He caught Juan's eye but whether or not the boy understood, he did not know. He considered taking him aside and asking him to say nothing to Catherine about what had happened, but the very thought of such an action struck him as being ridiculous.

Meanwhile, Catherine and Juan went into the garden. It was a cool, lovely evening with the moon in the sky. They sat together on a bench and Catherine yielded herself immediately to the boy's arms. She was filled with passion but Juan was passionless. He held her without warmth, and as she drew back away from him, she said,

"Forgive me—but I was worried. With you gone, I couldn't sleep. I could not sleep and I could not eat."

"Because I journeyed to Seville? That makes no sense, Catherine."

"Seville could be the other side of the world as far as I know. I've lived my whole life here in Segovia."

45

"Seville? Oh, it's just another place like Segovia, and we went there and now we are back."

"What happened there?" Catherine asked him.

"Well, you know what happened. I was presented to the Queen—"

"Did she adore you? What did she say to you? What is she like? You must tell me everything. At the Court of the Queen. Oh, that's exciting! Tell me what she was like."

"How many days is it to our wedding?" Juan asked, obliquely.

"Twenty-three."

As if he could not direct his thoughts or control them, Juan said, "There was a man there called Columbus. He was an Italian. He says the world is round, like a ball, and he intends to sail all around it—"

"What are you talking about, Juan? I know about him. My father told us about him. Didn't you hear what I said? I said it was twenty-three days to our wedding. Didn't you ask me that? We were talking about the Queen."

"The Queen hated me," Juan said bleakly. "What can I tell you about her?"

Then they sat in silence, Catherine puzzled and upset. Meanwhile, inside the house, Alvero and his wife Maria were arguing. They argued more and more frequently of late. It seemed to Alvero that some kind of acid was eating away at their relationship. When he was not with his wife, he felt that he needed her and wanted her and never had he felt it so desperately as during this trip to Seville. At the

46

same time, his disappointment matched his need. When they were alone, and he tried to explain to Maria how he felt about Torquemada, she refused to believe it.

"I will not believe it," she said, "I cannot believe it. It's not true, that's all, it's not true. You're being a fool, Alvero. You always become a fool over such things."

"What things?" he demanded. "You never think twice before you call me a fool, do you?"

"Don't shout at me, Alvero," she said primly.

"I am not shouting."

"Of course you are shouting. A gentleman does not raise his voice."

"Will you instruct me on the habits of a gentleman!" Alvero exclaimed. "Do you want me to go out of my mind? I am sick and worried and you instruct me on the habits of a gentleman?"

"I simply do not believe," Maria answered, "that anyone who loves us as much as Thomas does would turn against us—in any way. He is my confessor, so how could he turn against us? I have a right to my thoughts. I think you have just taken leave of your senses, that's all."

Pacing back and forth in front of her, Alvero said hoarsely, "You don't understand. My God, you don't understand at all. Now listen, just listen to me, Maria, listen. Torquemada said to me, Alvero—where do you come from? Those words. Just in those words, and suddenly those blue eyes of his were cold as ice. You understand me, like ice. He looked through me into my soul. That's the gift the man has. There

47

are no secrets in the world that are barred from him. This is why they made him Grand Inquisitor—"

Maria smiled and shook her head. "Alvero, he knows where you come from," she said patiently. "Haven't we spoken of it a dozen times? He knows that you come from Barcelona. Is it a secret?"

"Then why did he ask me?"

"He asked you a simple question, Alvero. I've never seen you this way before. I've never seen you so shaken. I don't know what you're afraid of."

"Of course you don't. I wonder whether you know what the Inquisition is. We go on with our lives, laughing, singing, pretending that the world is the way it always was, but underneath we know, underneath we know that there is a thing in Spain now, called the Inquisition, and day and night we are afraid, and this whole land stinks with fear."

"What a thing to say, my husband. Really, what a thing to say. How can you? I don't know how you can talk that way about Thomas. This is a man of God, who baptized our only child—"

Alvero came close to her now and dropped his voice to a whisper. "Just one thing, my wife. Do you know why he was summoned to Seville?"

"You told me," Maria answered primly. "King Ferdinand made him the Grand Inquisitor, the head of the Holy Inquisition. The more honor to all of us."

"My God—do you know what you are talking about?" Alvero asked her.

"There is no need to talk like that to me. I am no fool. Of course I know what I am talking about."

"Do you know what the Inquisition is? Or is it

48

because you know what it is that you can sit there, like a fool, and say the things you do?"

"How dare you call me a fool!"

"God help us!" Alvero exclaimed and then turned and strode out of the room.

Meanwhile, they were all of them in Torquemada's thoughts. Torquemada felt exalted, without fatigue and without fear. He had no desire to sleep, nor did he have any desire for company, and that night, as he often did, he walked in the pillared passageway of the cloister. The passageway was lit by intense silvery moonlight and in this moonlight, Torquemada paced the circuit of the cloister. Again and again he paced it, back and forth, filled with a strange kind of happiness at his own exaltation. It was not often that he felt exaltation. His was a somber and oppressed personality, but now he felt alive and excited—close to God—closer to God than he had ever been before.

CHAPTER FOUR

B<small>Y THE FOLLOWING MORNING</small> Alvero's mood had changed. Not only did a night's sleep and the bright sunlight of a new day make a difference, but this was the morning of a business meeting that Alvero had scheduled a month before. It had long been in Alvero's mind to make a compact between a group of merchants in Spain and groups in Italy and in the Netherlands. All three areas had completed a decade of enormous prosperity and Alvero believed that if the vast shipping capacity of the Netherlands and Milan were joined together with the military strength that the merchants of Spain could muster, a commercial triumvirate could come into being that would, in time, become a veritable empire.

He had fallen asleep to his thoughts and fancies of what it might mean if the Italian Columbus was right, and the westward route to the Indies could be opened; and now, this morning, as he greeted his associates, Hans Van Sitten and Salo Cordoza from the city of Amsterdam, Peri Gomez and Louis Lopez, both of them from Barcelona, and, finally, Dino Aleppo from Milan, he wondered what their reaction would be—and, in a light and amusing manner, he told them what Columbus proposed. Their interest belied his manner of telling. Alvero, sitting at the end of the long refectory table, dressed in sober black velvet and white shirt, olive-skinned, darkly handsome, combining the grace of a Spanish knight and the perspicacity of a merchant, was not to be taken lightly or dismissed; and immediately he had finished, Van Sitten, the Dutchman, asked him how much the Queen needed. Alvero replied that no figure had been established but that it was proposed to equip a small fleet of anywhere from four to ten ships, well armed, well provisioned and with ample goods for trade.

While Van Sitten calculated, Gomez explained that in spite of the years of prosperity that Spain had experienced, their gold supply had been drained through the constant wars with the Moors.

"It is a curious contradiction," Gomez said, "the surfeit of prosperity and the paralyzing shortage of coin. If this wild venture of the Italian results in anything, I pray that it will be bullion. We need it desperately. Right now in Spain every coin is counted—"

"Which I feel," Aleppo, the Italian, said, "is behind the growing power of your Inquisition—which seems to me to partake less of holiness than of greed. When you find a heretic, King and Church confiscate his property and worldly goods and divide them. Now this may enrich the King and enrich the Church, but believe me, Alvero, the effect is temporary and in the end you lose. You're eating your own flesh."

"Precisely." Van Sitten nodded. "You look to Amsterdam for the money. Is that so, Alvero?"

"Amsterdam and Milan." Alvero nodded.

"As far as Milan is concerned," Aleppo put in, "you can dismiss that. You can also dismiss Duke Sforza. If my words may be held secretly and in complete trust."

"In complete trust," Alvero said. "Believe me, my friend, what we say here goes no further. There is too much that we talk about that could be a noose around one man's throat or another's."

"Very well, then," Aleppo continued. "My own considered opinion is that the Duke of Sforza cannot and will not resist a French invasion. As far as the invasion itself is concerned, the King of France thinks and dreams of nothing else. The French are poor merchants and it is a simple fact of history that the less talented the merchant, the more often his thoughts turn to banditry."

"Nevertheless," Lopez put in, "it would seem to me that you are underestimating Sforza. Milan remains the richest city in Italy. Sforza can hire more mercenaries than Louis can. It's a simple matter of francs and florins."

"Not quite that simple," Cordoza put in. "Milan is rich, but believe me, friends, Milan does not generate enough money for Sforza to spend. At the same time, let us not forget that Sforza has a hundred thousand florins of our own money—at eight per cent, through Abraham Benalaph, the Jew of Amsterdam. I move that we persuade him to call the loan."

Alvero said quickly, "He has not defaulted. This would make an enemy of Sforza and Sforza still rules Milan, whatever the King of France plans."

"Which is exactly what Abraham will say, gentlemen. He will not call a loan of Sforza's. Every Jew in Europe would be at his throat if he did. Anyway, to my mind, Milan is less of a risk than Spain. There is a very good possibility that the King of France will honor Sforza's debts, even if he takes Milan. On the other hand, the King of France himself has been pleading for money and I suggest that we satisfy him to the extent of two hundred thousand florins at twenty per cent interest. That means that in three years the interest alone will cover whatever loss we incur with Sforza. We can act through the Jews in Paris and in Milan itself. On the other hand, if war is delayed, we stand to profit handsomely—"

"In so many words," Alvero said, "you suggest that we advance no money to the Queen of Spain. Isn't that the meaning of what you are saying, Van Sitten?"

"You tell me, Alvero, old friend, tell me yourself. They have made Torquemada the Grand Inquisitor now. Where does Spain go from here? Do you imagine that the Inquisition will ever be satisfied? Now, mind you, I talk among ourselves and only among ourselves—but, Alvero, is there a Spanish nobleman

who cannot find a little bit of Jewish blood, if not in
his mother and father, in his grandparents; if not in
his grandparents, in his great-grandparents? Where
does the Inquisition stop? What is a surety worth?
What is a guarantee worth? My own grandmother
was half-Jewish. Now I come to Spain as I would
come to an enemy land—"

For Alvero, the sunlight went away and the morning turned cold. By rote, he took part in the conversation and did what he had to do. But the zest had
gone. They finished their meeting and said their
farewells and all except Van Sitten left. Van Sitten
remained to lunch with Alvero. They were old
friends. At the luncheon table, Van Sitten was very
much the man of the world. He had traveled farther
than anyone Alvero knew and he entertained Catherine and Maria with his tales of faraway Russia, of
the Holy Land, of the wild Turks and the half-sav-
age Bulgarians. When the talk turned to Columbus,
Alvero found him agreeing with the contention of
Columbus that the Indies could be found by sailing
westward. Yet he held that the distance was, in
all probability, so great that no ship existed large
enough to carry the men and provisions all the way.
In Amsterdam, Van Sitten said, there were Jewish
geographers who had estimated the distance around
the world. It was much greater than the Italians
imagined.

"Curiously enough," Van Sitten said, "these are
your Spanish Jews. You've been sending us Spanish
Jews for two hundred years now, Alvero."

And then, seeing the expression on Maria de Rafel's

face, Van Sitten asked her whether it troubled her
to have him talk so openly about Jews. "The thought
of them is not pleasant to me," Maria said.

"Then I will not mention the name again," Van
Sitten apologized.

Afterwards, Alvero walked with Van Sitten to the
stables where Julio held his saddled horse. Before
he mounted, Van Sitten said to Alvero,

"I have seen you in better spirits, old friend. I
wish I could help you."

"Thank you. I am afraid no one can help me."

"As bad as that?" asked Van Sitten. Alvero
shrugged and Van Sitten said slowly, "It's two years
since I was last in Spain, Alvero. What has happened
since then?"

"You named it before—the Inquisition."

"Oh." Van Sitten studied Alvero thoughtfully for
a long moment before he said, "Your Jews should
have remained Jewish. They became Spanish noble-
men here. In Holland they remained Jews and we
live well with them. Here they are God's own temptation."

"You think God deals in temptation?"

"You Spaniards brood too much about God, Alvero. Too much about God and too much about
Jews."

"Both are our particular problem," Alvero said.
"You see, old friend, as you pointed out there isn't
a nobleman in this cursed country who isn't Jewish
—all Jewish, half Jewish, one-quarter Jewish, one-
eighth Jewish. We all call ourselves Christians now
but only dig the surface a little—" His voice died

away and he found himself staring at Julio, who was holding Van Sitten's horse a few paces from them.

"And you trust no one," Van Sitten said. Suddenly Alvero thrust out his hand at Van Sitten, took the Dutchman's hand and held it tightly. "Make this your last visit to Spain," he said softly.

"Then come to us," Van Sitten said.

Alvero stared at him without replying. Van Sitten mounted. Alvero took his reins and waved Julio away. Slowly, with great formality, Alvero walked the horse to the gate. Alvero said nothing more and, a moment later, Van Sitten rode off.

CHAPTER FIVE

AS VAN SITTEN RODE AWAY, standing by the horse gate, Alvero saw a man approaching his house. The man walked with slow dignity and around him there circled half a dozen ragged children, who pelted him with clods of dry dirt. For a moment Alvero did not recognize the Rabbi Mendoza and it occurred to him that he apparently lacked the ability to see the rabbi immediately as he was—as a rabbi and a Jew. But this time Alvero did not go to his aid; instead Alvero drew back behind the post of the horse gate and watched Mendoza approach the house. He remained hidden there in silence while Mendoza walked through the garden toward the front entrance—and then Alvero went quickly around the stables, approaching the house from the other direction. He stood at the edge of the gallery, outside and invisible to those within as Julio opened the door for Mendoza. Julio stared at the rabbi with astonishment—at first simply stood and stared while Mendoza faced him, and then somehow found his wits and moved aside and nodded for the Jew to enter.

Now, for a few steps, Mendoza's progress was invisible to Alvero. Catherine and Maria were at the other end of the gallery. Maria had cut some fabric that Alvero had brought back with him from Seville into a pattern for an overdress, and Catherine was helping her join the seams and pin them together. Both women were intent upon their work and therefore they did not see Mendoza as he entered the long gallery. He took a few paces which brought him into Alvero's area of vision and then he stopped. There he stood, his hands pressed together, his wide-brimmed hat on his head. It was evident to Alvero that Mendoza was unable to speak, unable to announce himself or to command the attention of the women—or afraid to, which would amount to the same thing. Now Julio joined him, looking at the Jew peculiarly and wondering, certainly, what his own role was to be in this affair. Alvero asked himself why he didn't go inside and put things at ease; yet, like Mendoza, he was frozen where he was, unable to move, unable to speak. Julio was only a servant. He finally shuffled down the gallery and stood in front of the women. Still they did not look up.

"Señora," Julio said.

Catherine was sitting to face the rabbi. Maria looked up at Julio, who pointed in the other direction and then Maria turned slowly. Both women then stared at Mendoza, both of them silent and

unmoving as if gripped with enormous astonishment
that was not unmixed with fear and repulsion.

To Alvero it was like witnessing a play, a scene on
stage. He felt detached and strangely objective about
his wife and daughter. Their astonishment angered
him; their fear annoyed him and to a degree dis-
gusted him; yet he too was unable to move or
speak.

Now, with the women watching him, Mendoza
took a few steps toward them and bowed slightly.
He was without courtliness or grace in a land that
set high esteem by them. He kept his hat upon his
head. His voice, however, was rich and his Spanish
strangely beautiful as he said, "I am the Rabbi Benjamin Mendoza. I took the liberty to come here. I
know that this was a great liberty to take with you
two noble ladies and I mean no annoyance—no pain
to you—I mean no difficulties for you—"

Maria found her voice. She sounded shrill and
defensive. "What do you want here?"

"Only to see Don Alvero, noble lady. Only to see
him and to speak with him."

As if aware of the shrillness of her voice, Maria
controlled it and turned it cold and flat as she asked,
"Have you an appointment with him?"

"No, I am afraid not. You see, how could I make
an appointment with him—unless I came here myself? I could not send another Jew here—you understand that. Who would I send here? I know that I
am an intruder, but I had to come myself."

"Then I am sure Don Alvero will be unable to see
you," Maria said.

"I can understand that. I mean I can understand that he would not want to see me. I am trying to say to you, noble lady—I know you to be his wife—that I am not wholly a fool. There are many things implicit in my coming here, but more important than that is the fact that Don Alvero de Rafel saved my life. He has a vested interest in me, so to speak, and we are a people peculiar about such things."

Now Maria rose and turned to her daughter and asked her to leave the room. Something was happening in Catherine that Alvero could almost feel physically. She tried not to look at her mother, who said, "I asked you to leave, Catherine, please."

"I want to stay."

"I don't care what you want. I asked you to leave, Catherine. Please leave."

Catherine shook her head, then suddenly her resistance collapsed. She got up and ran into the house. Maria was white and shaking with controlled anger, and now she turned to the rabbi and demanded of him,

"Who saved your life? Are you trying to tell me that my husband saved your life? What do you mean?"

"Only that he saved my life," the rabbi said.

"I heard you before. I heard you say that before. Who sent you here? Why did you come here?"

The rabbi shook his head and spread his hands. He was bewildered and amazed and unable to cope with the situation and he pleaded with her as he said, "If you came to my house, Doña Maria, I would

66

welcome you but I would not ask you why you had come."

Maria took another step toward him. "That I should come to your house, Jew, is inconceivable, inconceivable. It is more likely, to my way of thinking, that the sun will not rise in the morning. Inconceivable, do you understand me?"

Alvero could stand no more of this. He ran into the room, crying out, as in pain, "Maria!"

Perhaps the agony in his cry brought Catherine back. She stood at the far end of the gallery, half in the room, half hiding. Julio too could not pull himself away and stood watching—as if the outcome of all this were so unpredictable that life and death might depend on his being there.

Maria stared at her husband, then said to him with great calm, "This Jew asked to see you. He claims you saved his life. I told him that for him to have any reason to be here is inconceivable."

"This Jew," Alvero whispered. He went to Mendoza but could find no words for what he wanted to say. Then he walked over to his wife and whispered to her, "Maria—Maria—why don't you put a knife into my heart? A man comes into our house. The man is the Devil. He comes into our house. Then I say he is a guest. He is under our roof. Do we whip him? Do we insult him? Do we make him a thing of contempt?"

"You were listening," Maria said.

"I heard you from outside."

"You were listening," Maria said. "How could you? How could you stand out there and listen?"

"Is that all you can think about, that I listened to you?"

For a long moment Maria stared at her husband. Then she turned and walked the length of the gallery to the door where her daughter stood, walked past her and out. Catherine came into the room. She was crying now. She came a few more paces into the room and stood there. The old servant, Julio, came over and touched Alvero's velvet doublet.

"I am an old man," Julio said, "and I would rather die, Don Alvero, than to have you look at me the way you look at me."

"I trust you," Alvero whispered hoarsely.

"Say that in truth," Julio said, "or I will walk out to the stable and put a knife in my belly."

"In truth," Alvero whispered.

During this, Catherine had walked firmly to the table where a carafe of wine and glasses stood. She poured a glass of wine and, with great deliberation, her face set and intent, brought it to Mendoza and held out the glass to him. When, at first, he made no movement to accept it, Catherine said,

"Drink the wine of our household, Don Mendoza."

Alvero watched them. Mendoza took the wine and Catherine drew a chair from the table, nodding for him to sit down.

"Shall I drink alone?" Mendoza asked.

"Pour me a glass," Alvero told his daughter and then he said to Julio, "Bring us bread, Julio."

"The wine is enough," Mendoza said.

"It is my house," Alvero said almost bitterly. "If you drink wine here, you will break bread with me."

Alvero went over to his daughter, kissed her and whispered for her to leave. She nodded and went out of the room. Like two men in a tableau, Mendoza and Alvero stood silently, holding their wine glasses until Julio returned with the bread. Then Alvero broke the bread and offered some to the Jew, who chewed it thoughtfully as if he savored the taste of it.

"Please sit down," Alvero said to the rabbi.

Mendoza seated himself at the table and Alvero sat down facing him. Mendoza then spoke of Alvero's daughter. It seemed to Alvero that he quoted or paraphrased some words from the Bible but Alvero was not sure. He did not know the Bible very well. "You are blessed," Mendoza said, "you have a remarkable daughter."

"I suppose that is true, but remember that a blessing can be a curse. I love my daughter more than anything on earth."

"Love is never a curse."

Julio, who had stood there until now, suddenly turned and walked out of the room, and Mendoza said to Alvero,

"The man loves you. Why are you afraid of him, Don Alvero?"

"We are in Spain, Rabbi. Therefore we must learn to live with fear."

"There you have a curious proposition indeed, Don Alvero, for all Spaniards are not Jews."

"I don't understand you."

"I mean that the art of living with fear is a peculiarly Jewish art. Nevertheless, one must not be

69

afraid. If you live with fear and you are afraid, then you are right, Don Alvero—love will become a curse, but you can live with fear and be without fear, and then any love is a blessing. Why am I talking like this? I did not come here to discuss philosophy with you. In fact, I am sorry that I came here. It was the thoughtlessness and the greed of desperation that drove me here."

"I have nothing to forgive you for," Alvero said.

"Not even for saving my life?" Mendoza asked.

"Must I forgive you for that? I don't understand you. You were in danger and I did for you what I would do for any human being. It is not deserving of gratitude, nor is it worthy of discussion. It is a small thing."

"Not for me," Mendoza said softly.

"No, I did not mean that, no. Now you must forgive me."

"You are a strange man, Don Alvero, but it may be that all Spanish dons are very strange men. You, all of you, share a courtliness and a grace which is like a benediction. I think that is why it hurts so much when I see you afraid."

"Then I tell you that I am not afraid. God help me, I cringe in fear because a Jew enters my house! Are you a man of God, Rabbi?"

"You have your own men of God, Don Alvero."

"Then you offer me no comfort."

"I guess not," Mendoza agreed. "I came here to find comfort and not to bring comfort and I think for that I am sorry—and, if I have your leave, I will go and ask no further favors from you."

"What favors, Rabbi? What can I do for you?"

"You have done enough for me. Does it make you forever my debtor because you helped me once?"

"Perhaps."

"Then I have endangered you enough, simply by coming here, and thus all debts are paid," Mendoza said.

"Why did you come here?"

"Must I tell you?"

"I think so." Alvero nodded. "I sleep poorly as it is. Shall I sleep less poorly?"

"Very well," the Jew said, "you are a friend of Torquemada."

"How do you know that?" Alvero asked. "Because I was with him?"

"All of Segovia has known it for years."

"Then I am his friend." Alvero shrugged. "He is human, he feels, he suffers and he too sleeps poorly —whether or not you believe that."

"I believe it."

"He is a man and he needs friends. You are right, we have been friends many years."

"Then you know that he has decided to destroy our synagogue—to burn it to the ground."

"No! That is nonsense. Why should he?"

"Aren't there reasons enough, Don Alvero? Couldn't you itemize them, Don Alvero? He hates Jews. All right, you will reply to me that many people hate Jews. But he is also the Grand Inquisitor now—the head of the Holy Inquisition in all of Spain."

"That gives him no right to act against Jews," Alvero said, "or to destroy the synagogue. You know that. The Inquisition can take action against heretics, backsliders, blasphemers, but not against Jews."

"Rights, wrongs, you have a desperate need to think legalistically, haven't you, Don Alvero? But it is power that counts. He talks, he preaches. He calls for a punishment upon a pestilence. He is a righteous man, your Torquemada, and out of his righteousness he states what God wills. That is the curse of all righteous men. They talk with God's voice and Torquemada convinces too many people that it is God's will that the synagogue be burned to the ground."

Alvero stared at Mendoza—regarded him morosely and uneasily but said nothing. Mendoza sat for a little while, and then began to rise, asking Alvero, "Shall I leave you, Don Alvero?"

"Only if you wish." Alvero shrugged.

Mendoza was standing now. He shook his head and appeared to shiver. He stood there in silence for a moment or two and then he said to Alvero, "If you feel that on my part I should be aware of how small a thing a building is, compared to a human life, then I suppose you are right. I invest my synagogue with qualities it does not have. It is a very old synagogue, and we tend to confuse that with holiness, so we say that it is a holy place, a place that God remembers. It has stood here in Segovia for two thousand years. The Carthaginians built it. There were a great many Jews among the Carthaginians. Many reputable scholars believe that the Hamilcar family was Jewish and I once saw an old shred of parchment which said things that proved, in effect, that Hannibal himself had worshiped in our sanctuary. There is an inscription in the stone which says, in the old Aramaic, 'Here sacrificed Hannibal to the God of his fathers, to the God of Isaac, Abraham and Jacob,' but you never know whether such inscriptions are true or simply the result of legends that build up until someone believes them and feels that they must be inscribed in stone—"

Alvero rose now, facing the rabbi, and, speaking hoarsely, argued that a synagogue was a building, no more and no less. "Houses are built and houses are destroyed!" Alvero cried.

"I know, I know."

"The devil you do!" Alvero shouted. "I can't help you. Do you understand that? I don't think you understand what you are asking me. Do you know what you are asking me? Do you actually know what you are asking me to do?"

"Yes, I know," whispered the rabbi.

"Why did you come to me? Why me, out of the whole city? Suppose we talk to each other frankly and forthrightly. I have done business with Jews. There isn't a merchant in Spain who hasn't and I know how your people work. You buy and you sell and you bribe. You have bribed the City Council of Segovia a hundred times. You have bribed the priests. You have bribed bishops. Why come to me? Take up a collection of the money you need and your synagogue will stand. But why come to me? Why pick me out of all Segovia? Because I saved your life?"

"No, not because you saved my life."

"Of course because I saved your life. This makes me your slave, doesn't it? Your willing servant. Unwittingly and unknowingly I saved the life of one Jew—and now I must save the lives of a thousand Jews or of a synagogue or of anything else your fancy directs you to—"

"Only give me leave to go, Don Alvero," the rabbi begged him.

Alvero grabbed the rabbi's arm and swung him around to face him. Close to him, Alvero said, "Why me? Out of all Segovia, why me? Not because I saved your life. There is another reason."

"Must you have another reason?"

"I must," Alvero whispered.

"Very well, then"—Mendoza nodded, his voice soft, so soft that Alvero had to strain toward him to hear it—"I will give you the reason. In Barcelona I knew your father. I knew who he was and what he was. I loved him and I trusted him and I said that what he was must live on in his son."

74

CHAPTER SIX

AFTER MENDOZA LEFT, Alvero changed his clothes, put on riding boots and his sword, and sent word to the stables for his horse to be saddled. As he came down from his room, having seen nothing of his wife, Maria, since Mendoza's departure, he found Catherine waiting for him. She asked where he was going and he parried her questions. She took his arm and walked with him and Alvero said to her,

"You grow more beautiful each day."

"And you become more handsome each day," she countered. "Shall we go on praising each other? I would rather we didn't have to. It hurts when you quarrel with my mother."

"We had no quarrel," Alvero said, shortly.

"Why does she hate Jews?" Catherine wanted to know.

"Many people hate Jews."

77

"I don't hate them. Are they so very evil?"

"Like all people"—Alvero shrugged—"some are good and some are bad."

"And this man, this rabbi, Mendoza, that was his name, wasn't it? Tell me, is he good or bad?"

"Do you want me to judge men? I saw him once on the road when I helped him and again today at the house. We spoke for a little while together. That is not long enough to know whether a man is good or bad. A lifetime is not long enough to know that."

"What is a rabbi? Is he a priest?"

"Not exactly."

"What do you mean, not exactly? Don't you know what a rabbi is?"

"Yes, I know."

"Then why won't you tell me?"

"I am not trying to conceal things from you. I suppose he is like a priest or like a teacher, something of that sort—" He turned, almost abruptly, from his daughter and strode over to where Julio held the reins of his horse. As Alvero mounted, Catherine went to him. "I'll be back this evening," he said. She stood there, staring at him.

"What are you looking at?" Alvero demanded.

Catherine smiled suddenly. "You are a very handsome man, Don Alvero. Now why didn't that ever occur to me before? You are old but very handsome."

Alvero reared his horse around and spurred it away. He rode toward the outskirts of the town at a hard gallop, conscious that his daughter was watching him; but when he was out of sight of the house, he slowed the horse to a trot and then to a walk. Van Sitten, from whom he had parted some hours before, must have stopped at an inn in Segovia, because now Alvero saw him riding up ahead in the distance and he shouted to him and spurred his horse. Van Sitten reined up, recognized Alvero and waited until Alvero joined him. On the edge of town now, the road ran through an alleyway of old olive trees. In the distance peasants were working in the fields under the afternoon sun and there was a clear, steel-blue sky overhead. Van Sitten mopped his brow and said to Alvero,

"You know we dream of the sunshine, we Hollanders, but I think that after a few days in Spain, one has enough of it. God, it's hot! It doesn't seem to affect you at all."

"One gets used to it," Alvero replied. "Where are you off to now, good friend?"

"France and then home."

"I noticed before," Alvero said, "that you are in a hurry to leave Spain."

"I become afraid in Spain," Van Sitten said. "It's not a good feeling."

"Fear is a crazy master," Alvero said.

"So is death."

"You are not facing death."

"I think Spain is," Van Sitten said. "I think Spain is dying. I think that if you had an ounce of sense, Alvero, you would ride with me."

Alvero shook his head, but remained silent. They rode on together and Van Sitten continued to argue his point. He said that if only Alvero would come with him, he would wait until tomorrow and Alvero could make arrangements for his family. His fear was now on the edge of sanity and Alvero did his best to calm him. At last they came to a parting of the ways. The road to the north took a left-hand fork and the Priory of Torquemada lay a half mile to the right. They shook hands and said goodby. Alvero sat on his horse and watched Van Sitten ride away. Once Van Sitten stopped and turned and looked at Alvero, and, in reply to his unspoken question, Alvero shook his head. Then Van Sitten rode on and presently a bend in the road hid him from sight. Alvero spurred his horse and rode toward the monastery.

The monastery stood on flat land, surrounded by great gardens of fruit trees, olive trees and grape vines. Their robes hitched up to uncover their legs to the knees, their sleeves rolled back, the brown-skinned, bald-pated monks worked in the gardens. They hardly glanced up as Alvero passed by, and he rode his horse through them as if he and they occupied separate planes of existence.

Alvero dismounted and led his horse toward the cloister, where there was a tremendous hitchstone with iron rings set in its side. He tied his horse and walked through the cloister to the wooden doors of the monastery. Right now, the place was inhumanly silent, the only sound being the scraping of the mattocks of the working monks as they dug in the soil. Alvero opened the heavy wooden doors and entered.

At first after he had passed through the doors, he walked in Stygian blackness. He stood for a while,

waiting for his eyes to accustom themselves to the
dark, and then he made his way on until, turning a
corner, he found a long, shadowed passageway, lit
by broad beams of light let in through glassless windows. He stood waiting there for a moment, the light
playing over his hands and wrists, and then a monk
appeared at the other end of the passageway and
came toward him. The monk walked slowly through
the passageway until he was a few feet from where
Alvero stood. Then the monk waited in silence,
neither questioning nor suggesting.

"I want to see Father Thomas," Alvero said.

The monk appeared to think about this for a while.
The monk was a bald, brown-skinned man with a
thick neck and a flat, peasant face. He was of the
type who is as old as the soil of Spain itself, and as
fixed in perseverance, and as untroubled emotion-
ally. After he had thought about Alvero's request
sufficiently, he nodded and beckoned for Alvero to
follow him, and then he led Alvero down the passageway to a door that was marked with a purple
cross. The monk made a sign for Alvero to wait, and
then he opened the door and went into the room.
Half a minute later he was back and nodded for
Alvero to enter; and after Alvero had entered, the
monk, remaining outside, closed the door behind
him.

Alvero found himself in an austere room, about
thirty feet wide and some twenty feet deep. The
door through which he had entered was placed at
about the center of the room's width. Facing the
door, high on the wall, was a row of windows which

were glazed in colored glass. The strange light cast from these windows flowed across the depth of the room toward the door and gave the interior of the room an unearthly appearance. The walls were of stone, as was the floor, and at the far left, covering almost the entire wall, was a great crucifix, Christ's figure carved out of wood and hanging in a timeless and unendurable agony of pain.

The room was furnished with a long refectory table and, behind this table, facing the door, were seven high-backed chairs, each of them upholstered in black leather and each of them topped with a cross. On the table itself were two enormous brass sconces holding very thick candles. The candles were not lit now, the window light making any other illumination unnecessary. Also on the table was a large leather edition of the Vulgate Bible, a cross and rosary and some scrolls of parchment. In the center chair Torquemada sat, his chin on his hands, his eyes fixed on the table in front of him. Alvero entered, and still Torquemada did not look up; so Alvero stood there for a while and Torquemada sat behind the table and stared at the table. Then very slowly Torquemada raised his eyes and met Alvero's gaze. Still he did not speak and Alvero said to him very slowly and precisely,

"I met a man who said that Spain was dying."

"And you came to tell me." Torquemada nodded.

"No," Alvero said. "Once I would have come to you—not to tell you—but to ask you a great boon. I would have genuflected. I would have pressed my lips against your knuckles and said to you, give me faith to face such a thing."

"A man makes a foolish statement and you would ask for faith?"

"There is sometimes more truth in fools than in wise men."

"And sometimes more foolishness." Torquemada smiled. "A land does not die because a man says so. Shall I give you faith, Don Alvero?"

"We were friends once. When did it stop?"

"Did it stop, Don Alvero?"

"The time came and it stopped."

Then Torquemada said, "Tell me when, Don Alvero, tell me when that time was."

Alvero nodded and said, "If you wish me to, I will tell you. The time came when you knew what you must do—when you became a righteous man, Father Thomas."

"That says nothing, Don Alvero, except that you are quite clever. You specify then that I became a righteous man. You are a very clever man and I never underestimated you. Evidently you would commend a priest who lacked righteousness. That is most interesting indeed. But is it to tell me this that you come here without waiting for me to send for you?"

"I am a tortured man, Thomas. Is that a sign of cleverness, to be a tortured man? I admit to it. I am also not very clever. What game are you playing with me?"

"No game."

"What then?"

"Do you desire to confess yourself?" Torquemada asked softly.

"To the priest or to the Grand Inquisitor?"

"Both are the same man." Torquemada shrugged.

"I think not. I knew the priest."

"But I still know you, Don Alvero," Torquemada said dryly. "I know you better than you imagine."

"Better than I know myself?"

"It may be, it may well be that I know you better than you know yourself. I know many things, Alvero. I know, for example, that the Rabbi Benjamin Mendoza came to your home today."

"You waste no time to spy on me, Thomas!" Alvero cried.

"The Holy Inquisition does not spy," Torquemada replied quietly. "It sees. Who else will open his eyes to see? Would you do away with the Inquisition and let us all be blind? Has it never occurred to you that if Spain is dying, it is the Jew who chokes the life out of Spain?"

"I have always been taught that the Holy Inquisition is a churchly court and not concerned with Jews."

"That is pure sophistry, Don Alvero, and hardly worthy of you. The Holy Inquisition is concerned with Christians who are not Christians except in word and we are deeply, deeply concerned with the souls of these Christians who Judaize, who practice the Jewish rite in secret and who put their immortal souls in terrible jeopardy. As for the Rabbi Mendoza, I know why he came to you."

Alvero listened and asked himself whether he was

afraid. He said to himself, how much fear have you, Don Alvero de Rafel? You are a Spanish knight and yet the horror of fear is all over you. You are a Spaniard and a stranger here and what will you say to this man, Thomas de Torquemada?

Aloud, Alvero replied, "His synagogue is very old."

"Are those your arguments, Alvero?" Torquemada asked, raising a brow. "Do you plead for antiquity and the virtues of antiquity? The synagogue is old but so is the Jew, very old indeed. To destroy the one, you must destroy the other. So long as there are Jews, Christians will Judaize. Did you come to plead with me for the synagogue?"

With a sudden and impetuous earnestness and forthrightness Alvero said, "I haven't that much courage, Thomas. I am afraid. There is my confession. A Spanish knight pleads fear and horror. But tell me, who is there in all of Spain today who will plead for the survival of a synagogue?"

Smiling suddenly, Torquemada shook his head. "Alvero, Alvero—you surprise me."

"Answer me," Alvero insisted stubbornly.

"Answer you? Who will plead for a synagogue? The answer is obvious, Alvero. A Jew."

"Which I am not!" Alvero cried.

"Which you are not," Torquemada agreed dryly, nodding. He reached for one of the scrolls, opened it and stared at it for a while. "But you have a business associate, one Hans Van Sitten, a Hollander— with enough Jewish blood in him to confess to all things. Here in Segovia he entered the synagogue

85

when the Jews were at prayer. Did you know that I have four reputable witnesses who will swear that he Judaizes?"

"I don't believe that!"

"Reputable witnesses," Torquemada went on, "Spaniards, and they will swear to this and you tell me you don't believe it?"

"He is a Hollander."

"Will you bind the immortal soul around with national lines? Does being a Hollander exempt him from God's will? He is a friend of yours, yet will you keep him from the only thing that could purify him, that could give him hope—not in his moment here on earth but in all time?"

"What thing?"

"The stake," Torquemada said. "You are horrified?"

"Yes, I am horrified," Alvero admitted.

"Do you think it is easy to burn a human being alive? But, my dear Alvero, I am more horrified at the thought of a soul imperiled. Do you agree?"

There were no words left for Alvero. He stood there, silently staring at Torquemada.

"You spoke of friendship before, Alvero. I will open my arms and my heart but shall I weaken my faith for you?" He lifted one hand and directed his finger at Alvero. "I tell you this. Bring me proof that Van Sitten is a heretic. Denounce him before the Holy Inquisition. Then I will open my arms to you. Then I will listen to you. Then I will heed your requests, your pleas."

86

Still silent, Alvero stared at Torquemada, who said,

"I ask you only to prove yourself a Christian."

Alvero swallowed. He summoned the words and forced them to the surface and managed to whisper, "I must prove that to you?"

"Not to me. To God," Torquemada replied.

CHAPTER SEVEN

ALVERO CAME OUT of the monastery and stood at the door for a few moments, breathing deeply. It was late afternoon now and a great flight of herons, on their way to the heronry, winged across the sky. As Alvero watched them, a hawk broke up their formation and he wondered whether, somewhere, gentlemen were out hawking. How he envied them! He felt that such thoughts were odd, when another part of his mind was so deeply depressed.

Then he walked through the gardens toward the hitching stone. He passed among the monks, who continued with their work and paid no attention to him. In this silent place he was a silent and invisible person and still silent he stood by the hitching stone. Then he mounted and walked his horse away from the monastery.

The silence became even more enormous. It lay

upon the fields and upon the dusty hills in the distance. Alvero opened his shirt and, from under his shirt, brought out a silver chain. On this chain there was a cross and a tiny cylinder of silver. Each nestled against the other. He fingered them curiously, let them lay in his palm for a moment and then put chain and cross and cylinder back into his shirt. He was on the road that runs north from Segovia now, but of this fact he was hardly conscious. His horse walked slowly, the reins dangling loosely, and on the horse Alvero sat, bent over in his own thoughts. His thoughts sheltered him, encased him in a second ampule of silence within the greater silence that stretched around him in every direction. The road took an upward slope and the horse walked more and more slowly. At the top of the slope the horse came to a halt and still Alvero sat there, unmoving in the burning afternoon sun.

His eyes were on the stretch of road that ran north from where he was, and while he saw the road, he also did not see it. Two men in armor appeared upon the road, riding slowly toward Alvero. They were hard-faced men, wearing cuirasses and thigh-plates and they rode heavy-footed horses. Attached to the pommel of the saddle of one of them, there was a rope. The end of the rope was fastened around the neck of Van Sitten.

As they came closer, Alvero saw them—as if, sitting in a theater, the curtains were suddenly drawn apart—he saw them and he recognized Van Sitten. Van Sitten's hands were tied behind his back. His clothes were torn and from head to foot he was

covered with dust and blood. Every so often the
horseman to whose pommel the rope was tied would
whip his horse up into a sharp trot. When this happened, Van Sitten would try to run and keep pace,
but he would fall and be dragged by his neck, clutch
the rope with his hands, stumble to his feet, run
again, fall again and run again. Each time, when
Van Sitten was at the point of being choked to
death, the horseman would stop and wait for him
to recover himself.

The two horsemen reined in close to Alvero and
saluted him, the way common men salute a Spanish
gentleman. They were clerical soldiers, employed
by the Inquisition, fat with overeating and too little exercise. Their hair was tangled and their body
odor lay around them like a thick cloud. They sat
on their horses, grinning at Alvero, and he in turn
sat on his horse in silence and watched. Meanwhile,
Van Sitten stumbled toward Alvero, moving his
mouth silently. He opened his mouth and closed
his mouth again and again. While Alvero was well
aware that he was attempting to speak, no sound
came out of Van Sitten's mouth. His mouth was too
swollen and dry for the words to pass his lips; but
to Alvero, his silence was a part of the greater silence—and through that silence came Van Sitten's
terrible silent scream for help, for mercy, for some
sort of intervention.

But Alvero could not intervene. Alvero could not
move. Mentally he drew his sword and laid on to
the two soldiers and rescued Van Sitten and took
Van Sitten home with him and gave him fresh

clothes and a fresh horse and then sent him on his way to escape. All this happened in Alvero's mind, as a sort of mental exercise, but in real life nothing at all happened; except that after an appropriate interval the two Church soldiers spurred on their horses, dragging Van Sitten away along the dusty road.

Long minutes passed. Alvero's horse kicked at the dust and moved restlessly and finally Alvero groaned. He heard his own groan as if from a great distance, a groan of worse agony than would have come from Van Sitten had Van Sitten been able to find voice. Then suddenly Alvero drove his spurs into his horse, raked him with his spurs until the horse was racing across the fields in a wild and frantic gallop.

Time ceased for Alvero. He rode the horse in a great circle, spurring it and whipping it and giving it no rest until at last the exhausted horse lost its footing and fell. Even as it stumbled, Alvero flung himself clear, hitting the ground and rolling over and over, and then finally lay with his face in the dirt, but unharmed. When he got to his feet a peasant stood a few feet away from him, watching him; but the peasant said nothing and made no move to help him. Alvero walked over to the horse, which was trembling, its mouth dripping lather, its hide hot and wet. Alvero took the reins and led the horse on as darkness fell, and he found the road with only enough light left to see its dim outline. Then Alvero mounted and rode back to Segovia.

Alvero was empty now. The emptiness was dry

and terrible and he felt weak and nauseous. He felt that his soul had left him and all inside his body was dead, a dead weight upon his belly and his groin.

When he was only a little distance from his home, someone hailed him and he turned to see Juan Pomas trotting through the darkness to join him. There was a rising moon, enough light for Pomas to see his condition. The expression on Alvero's face was such as to keep Juan from making any comment. They came to the stables together and dismounted, and the stablehand, taking their horses, remarked to Alvero,

"You rode hard, master."

Alvero stared at him without replying. Then Alvero said to Juan almost harshly, "Go inside and tell them that I am here. I go to change my clothes."

With that Alvero turned on his heel and walked off. In his own chamber, he stripped off his clothes and Julio came to him with water and a sponge. Julio sponged him in silence, and then Alvero dried himself and put on black hose, black breeches and a white shirt. Over all this, he donned a long, black robe. He said nothing to Julio but walked out of the room and went downstairs to the gallery. At the entrance to the gallery he paused, hearing Catherine's voice—high-pitched and filled with the excitement that was a part of her. She was telling Maria about her day—about her visit to a woman called Carlotta, who had a reputation in Segovia for making the best pepper cheese. Maria disliked pepper cheese, which she considered a food of the poor and unworthy of service at a gentleman's table, but

Catherine had acquired a taste for it from the servants. She had apparently established the fact that she bought the cheese over Maria's annoyance and protests by now and was telling her mother about a fight that Carlotta had been having with her husband. Catherine had witnessed the fight. With awe and excitement she said,

"—a terrible fight, Mother. She was screaming at him and accusing him of sleeping with two other women. He's ugly as sin anyway and I can't understand how a man so ugly would find two other women to have an affair with—"

"And you stayed and listened!" Maria cried. "How could you? Don't you have any pride?"

"Mother, it was not a question of pride, believe me, and I'm a grown woman. I know about those things. They don't shock me. I have heard the servants have worse fights and say worse things to each other. I was buying cheese, that's all, and if you want good pepper cheese, you must go to Carlotta—"

"Pepper cheese!" her mother exclaimed, "why must you be so obstinate always?"

"Mother," Catherine said, "we've been through all that about the pepper cheese. Don't you want to hear what happened?"

"You might as well finish," Maria said.

"Well, Carlotta called his mother a whore and his grandmother a whore and his great-grandmother a whore, and then she picked up that long knife she uses to cut the hard cheese, and she ran after him, all around that big table where they squeeze the curds, and then she saw me; but she didn't stop running, Mother, she never stopped running and she never paused and she screamed at me, 'Darling, you're a grown woman. Otherwise I would never permit a thing like this, or a miserable wretch like this man in the same room with you.' I mean, Mother, that she said something like that, but the astonishing thing was that she never stopped running and he never stopped running—"

At this point Maria saw Alvero and went toward him. Catherine was laughing. She was laughing so hard now she was unable to speak. She ran to her father and kissed him, as Maria demanded,

"Where were you? The dinner will be cold and spoiled."

Now Alvero entered the gallery and saw Juan standing a little distance away. Catherine stopped laughing, let go of her father and went over to Juan. The three of them stared at Alvero now. There was a difference in him that could not be accounted for by the way he was dressed. He felt the difference and said to them, almost rudely, that it was time they ate.

In the refectory, the meal was served and eaten almost in silence. This dining room was smaller than the gallery, austere in the manner of the time, and lit by a chandelier containing thirty candles. Alvero loved the plain white plaster walls and the dark woodwork that framed the walls. In the center of one wall he had mounted a beautiful, round Moorish shield of brass—one of the finest pieces of brasswork he had ever seen, and which he himself had picked up on a battlefield twenty years before. The table was laid with white linen—as was always the case when they sat to dinner—and the plates were of silver, inlaid with gold. At this time, the knife and fork as twin table instruments had only newly been introduced to Spain. Those at Alvero's table were of iron, but the spoons were solid gold in the manner of the time. Alvero himself was unable to eat. The very thought of placing food in his mouth was impossible to him, and when Maria commented that he was eating nothing, he said only that he had a different kind of hunger.

"What happened today?" Maria demanded. "Where were you?" She would not be satisfied by the evasion of a question. She only repeated the question over and over again.

"I was riding," Alvero replied. Watching him closely, Catherine said that it was perfectly reasonable. She knew how much her father loved to ride and how he would use a horse to battle with whatever problems weighed upon him. Juan was silent and uneasy, and now and again Catherine smiled at him and nodded her head to comfort him and reassure him. A family storm was brewing and Catherine pitied Juan for being caught in the center of it.

"Yes, you were riding!" Maria exclaimed. "That answers everything, doesn't it? You were riding. I don't have to ask you where you were, what you did, who you saw. Your answer is that you were riding. You leave your food untouched and when I ask why, you answer me in riddles—"

"Our whole existence is a riddle," Alvero said

softly. He was very thirsty. He emptied his wine glass and now Julio appeared and poured wine into the glass until it was full again.

"What nonsense!" Maria snorted. "How can you speak such nonsense in front of Juan? We are a family. Juan is practically a part of our family. He came in and told us that your horse was wet and trembling with exhaustion."

"I ride hard!" Alvero snapped.

"When we need you," Maria said, "a horse takes the place of your family."

"Why do you need me? What happened here today?"

"While you were gone, the Prior was here," Maria replied.

"Torquemada?"

"I wasn't here," Maria said defensively. "He spoke to Catherine."

Alvero turned to Catherine now, who said placatingly, "Father, he only asked me why you wear a silver ampule on the chain around your neck. So you see what a small thing it was?"

Very gently Alvero said, "And what did you tell him, child?"

"I told him that you had always worn it." Catherine shrugged, and then asked him what it was. "You see, I don't know what it is, Father, or why you wear it. Why do you wear it?"

"It's only a memory," Alvero answered. "I shed myself of most of my memories but no one can cast away all of them. No one, not myself—not Torquemada." Alvero felt under his collar, found the chain and passed it over his head. He laid it down on the table in front of him, the cross and the ampule extended toward Catherine; and dryly and harshly Maria demanded of him,

"Alvero, what are you doing? What kind of a grotesque joke are you making of this whole thing? Torquemada came here to ask about that. Don't you have any sense?"

"I know that Torquemada came here to ask about it." Alvero nodded. "The good Prior extends his knowledge. There must be no mysteries for him. I am sure he has guessed what I wear about my neck. Have you never guessed, Maria? Have you never asked yourself why I wear this and what it is? Really, Maria—never once?"

Juan Pomas rose uneasily. Gripping the table, he attempted to excuse himself. He explained to Alvero that what was happening here now was a family matter and, while he would someday be a part of this family, he was not yet such a part. "So you will pardon me," he said. "I think I should go now."

"Not yet!" Alvero said coldly. "Sit down, Juan. You will leave when I tell you to leave." Then Alvero turned to Julio and said, "That's enough, Julio. We will be alone."

Julio bowed gravely and walked out of the room and then for a long moment the four of them sat in silence, while Alvero's hands played with the cross and the ampule. Catherine watched his hands, thinking about how strong and competent and long-fingered they were. Why had that never occurred to her before? Juan had collapsed into his chair and now sat staring at the table. Maria, annoyed and troubled, demanded to know why Torquemada had come to their house today. When Alvero did not answer her, she pointed to the ampule and cried,

"What is that thing, Alvero?"

"You ask me now—after twenty-two years?"

"Father," Catherine said, "for God's sake, what did happen today?"

"I don't know. I am not sure. Something happened but I am not sure. How can I explain that to you. This—" Now Alvero held up the ampule. "This thing belonged to my father and, before him, it belonged to his father. What is it? Like the cross, it is a holy thing. Inside of it there is a tiny piece of parchment, and on the parchment, a few words are written—"

"Stop! Enough!" Maria cried shrilly.

As if he had not heard her, Alvero turned to Juan and asked him whether he understood. Did he follow Alvero's meaning? Juan shook his head. He was puzzled and frightened.

Watching him, Catherine could only think of a trapped beast—and yet Juan was not a beast—far from it. A chicken in the slaughterer's hands; a dog with his foot in the trap; or a man drained of manhood. Catherine wanted to cry, to weep, to go down on her knees and plead with her father to stop this thing and let Juan go. But she said nothing.

Her mother rose and announced coldly, "I will not have this! I will not! I will not!"

Softly but bitterly Alvero said, "Sit down, Maria, sit down! Do you understand me? I said you are to sit down, Maria." Alvero nodded as his wife obeyed him and resumed her place at the table. "What will you not have? The Jew in you? The Jew in me? The Jew in Catherine? The Jew in Juan?"

Juan shook his head fiercely. He opened his mouth to speak, licked his lips and then shook his head again. His skin had become white as paste, and to Catherine it seemed that his dark eyes were staring out of a sort of death's head mask.

"What? Come, Juan Pomas," Alvero whispered. "Do you deny this?"

Totally unnerved, Juan sprang to his feet, leaned over the table toward Alvero and demanded pleadingly, "What are you doing, Don Alvero? In God's name, what are you doing to me? I am a Christian. You know that I am a Christian."

"A Christian?" Alvero asked, smiling. "Of course you are a Christian, Juan Pomas. Do I deny that? But your great-grandfather, Jacob Pomas, was a rabbi. Will you make a Christian of him?"

"I am a Christian," Juan pleaded.

Maria rose now, her face dark as the night, stormed away from the table toward the door of the refectory, halted then, turned back to Alvero until she was close enough for him to hear her whisper. She whispered to him hoarsely, "You are mad! You have lost your mind! You are mad! You are insane! You are a thing that they bind and put away!"

"Am I mad?" Alvero asked tiredly. "Really, Maria, do you think I am mad or am I simply practical? Is there a noble family in all of Spain without Jewish blood? Is there, Maria? Was your own mother half-Jewish or not?"

"Lies," Maria shouted now. "How do you dare to sit there and lie and blaspheme?"

Alvero nodded. "Yes, my dear wife. Our whole existence is a lie, a riddle, perhaps an epitaph. I don't know; I think we have a mortal sickness and we are dying. I think that Spain is dying too."

Alvero picked up the ampule and held it between his fingers. Her voice very calm, almost indifferent, Catherine asked him,

"What is that, Father? You say that it has a bit of parchment in it. Is anything written on the parchment?"

Maria and Juan did not move now. They were listening. Then, as Alvero began to speak, Juan sank back into his chair as if hope were fleeing too fast for him ever to overtake it.

"They call it the Jewish curse," Alvero said. "It is a thing that Jews put on the doorposts of their houses. It has this little piece of parchment in it and on the parchment in Hebrew letters it says, 'And thou shalt love the Lord thy God with all thy heart and all thy soul and all thy might.'"

Maria covered her face with her hands and began to sob. That way, sobbing, stumbling, half-blinded behind the curtain of her hands, she moved out of the refectory. When she had gone, the three sat in silence for a minute or two and then Catherine said to her father,

"Only that?"

Alvero rose. "Only that, my child—only that. I

must go to your mother now. She is deeply disturbed. I don't know why I did it to her. Believe me, I never did this to her before."

Then Alvero walked out of the refectory, but Juan and Catherine continued to sit at the table. Catherine reached across the table for the chain, picked it up and fingered the cross and the ampule. She played with these two things as she would have touched the beads in a rosary. Then Juan said to her,

"Catherine? Please, Catherine?"

"What is it, Juan?"

Juan did not answer, only sat there; and looking at him now Catherine asked him why he was afraid. She asked this very simply and very directly. "Why are you so afraid? Do you hate my father for this thing?"

Still Juan did not answer. Catherine held out the chain to him. He drew back as if it bore a dreadful threat in and of itself.

"I feel no different," Catherine said. "An hour ago I did not know that part of me was Jewish or that part of you was Jewish. Now I know it. I feel no different. No different at all."

The words burst out of him. "I am a Christian, as you are. You know that, Catherine."

"Yes, I know that. It means that I am both. I am a Jew and a Christian and still it seems to make no difference."

"No!"

Catherine put the chain around her own neck now and looked at Juan, who whispered fiercely,

"Take it off, please, please, for God's sake, take it off!"

Catherine smiled, holding the ampule in the palm of her hand. She said lightly, "And with this thing in my hand I Judaize. Now suppose that our good Prior Thomas was here. Then I would say to him, Father Thomas, I Judaize. Poor Prior Thomas. He would have to burn me. He would have to tie me to a stake and burn me—" Her voice died away. The brightness went out of her like a candle that has come to the end of its wick and darkens before it extinguishes itself. Then Catherine leaned toward Juan and whispered, "Oh my God, Juan, what has happened here?"

"Don't let it happen to us," Juan pleaded.

"When I was a little girl, Juan, they held a tourney of knights here in Segovia. It was the last one; I think the last such tourney in all of Spain. Today the world is different and people smile at such things. But then, for a little girl, it was very wonderful. All the Spanish gentlemen were in steel from head to foot, their banners and pennants in the wind. Such color as you can't imagine, one knight in bright red and another in sky blue and still another in the purest white. And then, in the joust, there would be a terrible clash of arms, of steel on steel as the riders came together—" She paused for a moment as if she had been bodily transported back into the scene. "My father rode in the tourney. Is it hard to imagine Don Alvero all in armor from head to foot? His color was white. All in armor with the white robe covering him. Do you know that he seemed to me to be the noblest knight in the world? He unseated the man he rode against and then he reared his horse and came around and trotted over to where I was and he reached down and lifted me to his saddle, in front of him—"

"Catherine, for God's sake, don't you understand what is happening? How can you prattle like this about knights in armor? Are you an idiot? Don't you know what is happening in Segovia? Not knights in armor. No knight in armor will rescue us from what is happening—"

"Do you still want to marry me, Juan?" Catherine interrupted, her voice cold and precise now.

"I have given my word."

In a sudden fury Catherine rose, took two steps away from the table and then turned to Juan Pomas and cried out, "Be damned with your word! I release you from your word!" And then she stalked out of the room, leaving Juan Pomas alone.

CHAPTER EIGHT

FOR JUAN POMAS there had been no sleep that night. He walked through the night, leading his horse. He tied his horse to a dead tree and sat on a rock and brooded and cursed himself and even wept a little. He sat like that for hours until he heard a cock crow, and then he mounted his horse and rode away through the darkness. As dawn approached, the darkness began to lessen and in the distance the bells of the monastery began to toll. Juan Pomas turned his horse's steps toward the sound of the bells.

Torquemada saw him approaching. As with Juan, Torquemada's night had been sleepless, but many of his nights were sleepless. At night Torquemada closed the door of his small, cell-like room behind him and then he fought the devil. Sometimes he stripped naked and called in a monk to whip him, to beat his flesh until he was covered all over with livid welts; and these welts were like armor in his battle against the devil. Torquemada was not always victorious. There were nights when he triumphed and there were nights when the devil triumphed; but always he returned to the battle. He had few doubts about who would be the final victor.

Now, as the bells above him tolled the end of the night, Torquemada walked slowly through the cloister. Each long step appeared to keep pace with the tolling of the bells, nor did he pause in his walk as Juan rode into the gardens of the monastery and hitched his horse at the huge, ancient hitching stone.

To Juan it appeared that Torquemada had not seen him; but this was a normal thing for those who approached Torquemada. He had taught himself to notice without noticing, to see without seeing and even to judge without judging. Juan walked over to the cloister and stepped into its deeper darkness, and he waited while Torquemada made another circuit. Returning on his way, Torquemada halted a few paces from Juan and stood there. In the shadow of the cloister, Juan Pomas was unable to see whether or not Torquemada was looking at him or how he was appraising him, or whether there was a question in Torquemada's eyes. Torquemada had no eyes, no face, only a cowled shape, a black robe that exchanged form with the form of the shadows that surrounded him.

The two of them stood there while the morning became gray and then a paler gray, and finally Torquemada observed softly,

"At this time, my son, so early in the morning, the

body may be clothed—but the soul is naked. To God, the soul is naked. It stands naked before God because no clothes and no body will cover it or hide it."

It was not a question and it was not a statement. Juan did not know what to say, so he simply waited and said nothing—only stood there, afraid and waiting. Torquemada went on,

"The night is a time for sleep. Why couldn't you sleep, my son?"

Juan Pomas shook his head dumbly. He was terribly afraid and he felt a desperate need to answer Torquemada's question, but he could not speak and he only shook his head dumbly.

"Do you fear me, my son?" Torquemada asked gently. "What is there to fear? We are the servants of God. People of Christ. How can you fear me? Have you heard it said that Torquemada was once a man and has now become a monster? Do monsters serve God? This is a question you must ask yourself and you must answer this question as well. Tell me, do monsters serve God?"

"I don't know," Juan muttered.

Now it was light, with the true morning light, and the first rays of the sun touched the flat towers of the monastery. Juan could see Torquemada now; his robe became a robe of black homespun, his face, cowled over, was an edge of jutting bone, an area of brown skin, a jaw sloping and bony, but still he had no eyes. The eyes were hidden deep in the shadow of his cowl.

"Will you serve God?" Torquemada asked Juan.

"Will you serve Spain? Will you serve your immortal soul?"

Juan tried to speak but no words came forth. He wanted to run away and he knew that flight was forbidden. He wanted to get down on his knees and plead for mercy, and that too was equally forbidden.

"Do you think that God has forgotten Spain?" Torquemada went on. "If that is what you think, then I must ask myself why you think such thoughts. I must ask myself why God's child and Spain's child should think that God has forgotten Spain. I must open my heart to you and I must give you answers —otherwise, I am no priest. So I say to you, my son, God has not forgotten Spain, God has only forgotten the Jew. In all the time between creation and now, God has only forgotten the Jew. But—"

He now came closer to Juan, so close that Juan was able at last to see his eyes, black pits in his hard-boned face.

"But the Jew who becomes a Christian—this Jew God remembers. For this Jew has an immortal soul and there is no immortal soul on this earth that God has ever forgotten."

He reached out his hand and touched Juan's shoulder and said, "Let us walk."

Juan walked beside him. There was nothing else that Juan could do, so Juan walked beside him and they moved around the cloister. For a while they walked in silence, until they came to the end of the colonnade. Then Torquemada turned about and they began to pace back over the path they had come. Then Torquemada said to Juan,

"What brought you here, Juan Pomas? Few come here of their own free will. They come more easily when the soldiers of the Inquisition—of the Holy Mother Church—when these soldiers bring them. But no soldiers of the Inquisition were sent for you —and yet you came."

Now Torquemada reached out and touched Juan's neck. His finger traced a line around Juan's neck, and the young man shivered and shrank away. Torquemada whispered,

"What is the ampule that Don Alvero wears around his neck?"

Torquemada walked on, waiting, and Juan walked with him. But from Juan there was no reply or comment. They reached the end of the cloister and once again Torquemada turned and began to pace back.

"The Holy Inquisition. Holy as the Father, the Son and the Holy Ghost. Their court is also holy. Do you know what the Holy Inquisition is, my son?"

Torquemada put his arm across Juan's shoulders. Juan pulled away suddenly and cried out to him,

"I swear by the Mother of God, as I am a Christian! I swear, I swear to you, Father Thomas, that Don Alvero is a Christian!"

Softly, calmly Torquemada whispered, "You swear too much. Why do you imperil your immortal soul? God hates an oath. Did I ask you to swear? Did I ask you that?"

"Don Alvero is a Christian!"

"You answer a question I never asked," Torque-

mada said. "We have the answer, but where is the
question, Juan Pomas? Is it in your heart, in your
soul, or is it God's voice? I did not ask you whether
Don Alvero is a Christian. I asked you what is in the
ampule he wears around his neck."

"A curse," Juan blurted out.

"What curse?"

"The Jewish curse."

"Tell me, Juan Pomas, what is the Jewish curse?
Do you know? And if you know, tell me how you
know."

"I heard Don Alvero speak of it."

"Of what?"

"I told you. I heard Don Alvero speak the Jewish
curse."

Torquemada nodded and resumed his walk. Juan
walked beside him as if some unseen force bound
him to the Prior. Finally Torquemada said, "Speak
this curse here, Juan Pomas."

Six more paces they walked and Juan remained
silent; and then Torquemada cried out, his voice
strong and commanding,

"I absolve you! I order you! On pain of my anger,
I order you to speak!"

Juan stopped and turned and faced him and said
to him pleadingly, "And thou shalt love the Lord thy
God with all thy heart and all thy soul and all thy
might."

The bells began to toll again. The voice of the
bells built up in Juan Pomas' head until he thought
that the force of this thunderous clangor would ex-
plode his skull and leave him mindless.

CHAPTER NINE

THAT MORNING Maria decided to go to church and Catherine agreed to go with her. Somehow or other Maria had built up in her mind a pattern of events—events that could be negated or extinguished simply by spending the morning in church. She tried to explain to Catherine how they would confess themselves and how many candles they would light and precisely what they would say to those two priests she most favored. Catherine listened but without enthusiasm or conviction, and when Maria put it to Alvero that he should go with them he shook his head angrily and tried to hurry them on their way.

Catherine was troubled. She said to her father, "Will you stay here? Will you remain here? Will you be here when we return?"

Alvero forced himself to smile and to reassure her.

"Mother wants me to confess," Catherine said.

"That's an excellent notion," Alvero agreed. "I think you should. You will feel better."

"Don't you remember?" Catherine whispered fiercely.

"I remember nothing that troubles me in any way —and certainly nothing that should trouble you," Alvero said. "Go to church and do as your mother wishes."

Alvero was relieved when they were gone. What he knew would happen, he expected to happen any moment now and each minute that went by without it happening was a sort of reprieve to him. He went into his own room, his private cabinet where he kept his ledgers and his accounts and where he did his own work, and he sat down at his desk and began to write. He had proposed to himself that he would write a single letter to his wife and his daughter together. When he could not find the words to get started upon this project, he attempted to write to Maria. That too proved an impossible task. Maria had left the house only a short while before, yet he could not evoke any image of her. There had been no parting between them. She had simply turned her back on him and walked out; but such an action was quite reasonable from Maria's point of view. There was no reason why Maria should consider that this morning was different from any other morning.

At last Alvero settled in his own mind for a letter to Catherine and once he began to write the words flowed easily from his pen. He had finished this letter, folded it and sealed it and was at work on a second document, a sort of codicil to his will, when he heard the sound of marching men and steel against steel outside in the street. He walked over to the window and there in the burning morning sunlight he saw six Inquisition soldiers marching down the street toward the house. They were in half-armor, their big boat-shaped helms tilted back on their heads. As always they were unkempt and their arms were poorly kept and Alvero found himself thinking that if he commanded them his first action would be to turn the lot of them into the river-bed with plenty of soap. The thought was childish and he shrugged and went back to his desk and to the document he was writing. One part of him concentrated on what he was doing. Another part of him heard the soldiers hammer at the door and then heard Julio's muffled voice as he opened the door. Presently Julio was tapping on the door to his room. Alvero rose and let the servant in.

"What is it, Julio?" Alvero asked.

"You know, don't you? You must have heard them."

"I know."

"I would not let them in the house," Julio said. "They are filthy and they stink. Anyway it is not fitting that such scum should enter the house of a Spanish gentleman and drag him away like a thief."

"And did they agree to wait outside?"

Julio nodded.

"For now," Alvero said. "Presently they will become bolder. They will stop knocking at doors and break down doors and when good people like yourself stand in their way they will kill without thinking twice about it."

"You must go with them?" Julio asked.

"For the moment, yes. Never mind that, there are more important things." He handed the letter he had written to Julio. "This is for my daughter, Julio. It is very important."

"She will have it, Don Alvero."

"Now this—" Alvero took up the second piece of paper and handed it to Julio. "This, Julio, is a codicil to my will. It says that if I should die you are entitled to the ownership of the white stallion you have always admired and also to one hundred gold pieces—"

"Please, please, Don Alvero," Julio interrupted. "I don't want you to talk about that. Your death is far away."

"No man's death is far away," Alvero said impatiently. "Now you just listen to me and take this document and do what I say. I know that you cannot read, Julio, but I have explained to you what is in the document. If you lose this document, you will be entitled to nothing except the little bit in my regular will. I want you to know that in my regular will I provide for you and for the other servants, but that is a small matter. I want you to have this. Now leave me alone and go to the holy soldiers and tell them that I will be with them as soon as I have dressed myself properly."

Alvero's shirt was stained with perspiration already. He put on a fresh shirt of white silk and over it a velvet vest. He buckled his finest ornamental dagger onto his belt, took his mirror, and combed his long hair carefully. As he walked to the door, he smiled, reflecting on the childish vanity of his own actions.

The Inquisition soldiers were waiting for him. The sergeant in charge of the small squad said to him,

"We will not put irons upon you, Don Alvero, but you must not try to escape. I know that we are dealing with a Spanish gentleman, but you will admit that these are different times."

"I admit that, Sergeant." Alvero nodded.

"Strange times, Don Alvero. It is not enough simply to be a Spanish gentleman or to be a sergeant like myself. All relationships have changed, don't you agree?"

"I agree." Alvero nodded.

"So I will not put the irons upon you and you must not try to escape. Just stand among us and we will all walk together to the priory."

Alvero nodded and took his place among the soldiers and they marched off. The church bells had stopped ringing now and the only sound was the clank of the soldiers' metal and the hard crunch of their feet. As they passed through the streets of Segovia, men and women and children paused in whatever they were doing to look at them. But no one said anything, no one laughed, no one mocked, no one spoke. Even the children were silent. There was no one in Segovia who did not know Don Alvero, but now no one had a word to say for him or a word to say against him.

That way they marched through Segovia and out of the town on the road that led to the monastery.

The morning was warmer than usual. By the time they reached the monastery, Alvero was perspiring again and he remembered how upset Maria would become when he ruined one of his very fine and expensive silk shirts with perspiration. No matter how much the peons rinsed the shirts in salt water, perspiration stains remained.

They walked on through among the monks, who went on with their work, neither watching them nor acknowledging their existence by any word or action. They went through the cloister and into the building and down the corridor to the Inquisition room. A black-robed Dominican was waiting and he nodded at the soldiers and told them to leave Alvero and to go. Then the Dominican opened the door of the Inquisition room and motioned for Alvero to enter. Alvero walked in slowly. The friar followed him, closing the door.

Now there were seven men at the long refectory table that stood in the center of the room. In the middle was Torquemada and on each side of him there were three Inquisitors. They were all of them strangely alike, not indulgent men, not fat men or cheerful men—but all of them strangely like Torquemada, lean of face, dark of eye, brown-skinned and determined. They stared at Alvero as he entered but their stares carried no particular meaning. They neither approved nor disapproved. They simply watched him.

At this time of the morning the light from the

windows behind the Inquisitors glared down in broad bands. The light lit up Alvero who stood in the midst of great shafts of dancing dust motes. The Inquisitors however remained shadowed, strangely distant, strangely aloof.

For Alvero at this moment, there was neither fear nor anger. If he had been asked to state precisely what he felt, he would have had to reply that he felt nothing at all. He was divorced from himself and it was with real rather than feigned curiosity that he said to Torquemada,

"Why have you brought me here, Thomas?"

"Don't you know?"

"If I knew I would not ask you."

"You see, Alvero," Torquemada said, "we have many years of friendship behind us. I know you very well—and I think that I know something about your soul, but your mind remains closed to me. I have no powers to enter it; I have no magic or unearthly skills. I am only a poor monk who does the best he can and I think that you know that better than anyone else. So suppose you tell me why you are here."

"I don't know."

"Don Alvero," Torquemada went on, "do you accept the doctrine of the immortality of the human soul?"

"I accept it."

"Then we are here not as your enemies but as your saviors—for what is any earthly discomfort as against the eternity of immortality?"

At this point Torquemada waited. He leaned forward eagerly and the three friars on either side of him looked from his face to Alvero's face and then back to Torquemada's face. But Alvero did not reply and then Torquemada said gently,

"Confess yourself."

"Of what?"

"Shall we decide that?"

"Tell me what I am charged with," Alvero demanded.

"As simple as that. Most men who stand here, Don Alvero de Rafel, are filled with fear. They don't fear me. They fear God, and in me they fear only what is God's purpose. Are you not afraid?"

"No."

"Do you fear God, Alvero?"

"I fear only what threatens me," Alvero answered slowly. "God doesn't threaten me."

"Do I threaten you?"

"I will not put boundaries on friendship, Thomas. There is no need for either of us to lacerate the skin or the soul of the other. Tell me what I am charged with."

Torquemada sighed and then suddenly clenched his fist and smashed it down on the table in front of him. "The supreme heresy! Judaizing!"

"I am no Jew, I am a Christian," Alvero said softly.

"So you are—so you are, Alvero de Rafel. Otherwise you would not stand before this Holy Inquisition. No Jew stands here—for to what purpose, to what end would they stand here? Damned as they are from the moment of their birth, they have no hope of salvation. Neither sin nor heresy is within

their province—only the perpetuation of God's curse
untempered by God's mercy. Such is the condition
of the Jew and the holy stones of this priory will not
be stained by his presence."

Torquemada's anger went almost as if he had ver-
bally dismissed it. His voice became gentle and understanding. His clenched fist opened and his fingers
traced patterns on the table in front of him. He
looked up at Alvero and his dark eyes probed search-
ingly as he said, "I have known you many years,
Don Alvero de Rafel—yourself and your wife and
your daughter. As an unbaptized infant I held your
daughter in the palm of my hand and I have
watched her grow. I have known you and I have
loved you. Do not place your damnation as another
burden upon me. I have burden enough. You said
before that we were friends and if that is the case
there is a necessity for understanding. Understand
the burden I bear, Alvero. I plead with you—confess
yourself, absolve yourself."

Alvero considered this thought and then nodded.
He felt strangely objective as he said, "So that you
may lash me to a stake and burn me alive?"

Now the Inquisitor to the far right of Torquemada, an old, old man, cried out, "The mortal body
is burned. Fire strengthens the soul. Only this dis-
ease we call life is burned away—"

And the man sitting next to him said, "The mortal
body—which is filth, dirt and sin. Do you hear, Don
Alvero?" The old man at the far right smiled. He
was almost toothless, a single yellow tooth in the
bottom of his jaw, two yellow fangs on top. It made

him lisp as he spoke. "The mortal body goes in purification. You lose it, Don Alvero, but think of what
you gain. The gain is life everlasting."

At the other side of Torquemada an Inquisitor
intoned, "Purged by fire of all sin, purged and pure.
Pure and full of grace, full of grace."

Torquemada shook his head impatiently and Alvero had the feeling that the Prior was both annoyed and embarrassed by the comments of his col-
leagues. "Become one with your God," Torquemada
said. "Give up your torment, Don Alvero."

"No, Thomas," Alvero replied. "My torment is one
thing I will not surrender easily."

Now the old man on the far left found reason to
be indignant and demanded how Alvero dared to
address the Grand Inquisitor in so familiar a manner.

"He despises us," another Inquisitor said. "It is
obvious that he despises us." And then addressing
himself to Alvero, "Do you despise us, sir?"

"I remembered a friend," Alvero said. "Do I sin
by calling him Thomas?" He addressed himself directly to Torquemada and asked for an answer.
"Does it go with my other sins? Shall I no longer
call you Thomas?"

"I too remember a friend," Torquemada said. "Call
me Thomas so long as you can, God help me—God
help both of us. I speak to you as a friend, Alvero.
Give up your torment and be at peace with yourself."

"But I have found something precious in my torment."

"Something precious? What have you found, Don Alvero?"

"Myself."

"As a heretic? As a Jew? How have you found yourself, Alvero?"

"As a human being."

"And what does that signify, Alvero? That you are a thing of flesh and blood? That you eat, that you sleep, that you breathe? An animal performs all those functions. An animal is flesh and blood. A Jew is flesh and blood. I was speaking before of your immortal soul."

"And if the body needs flesh and blood how does the immortal soul nourish itself? With mercy and pity? Or is all that I was taught a lie?"

"We are mercy and pity—ourselves, the Holy Inquisition."

"Mercy and pity," Alvero said, unable to keep the astonishment out of his voice. "Oh no, Thomas, you take me as a fool. You mock me and you play games with me."

"I offer you something precious."

"What do you offer me? A stake where I can burn? A prison cell where I can rot?"

Now the Inquisitor on the far right cried out shrilly and impatiently, "Our Lord hung from a stake. A stake will free you of your heresy. The purification of flames will be wrapped around you like a cloak —a cloak of love and thoughtfulness—"

Alvero could contain himself no longer and pointing to the old man he cried out at Torquemada, "Thomas, whatever I must endure before you I must endure, but I will not stand here and listen to that old idiot!"

Torquemada turned to the old man and said to him harshly, "Enough! No more from you!" Torquemada looked at the others. "All of you—leave it be or you will do penance sufficient unto my anger. This man stands before me and I will examine him."

"You go too far, Prior," one of the Inquisitors said.

"I will not have you tell me how far to go," Torquemada replied coldly and angrily. He turned to Alvero now and said to him harshly, "I pleaded with you, Alvero, but I can plead with you no more. Confess yourself!"

"I have no sins to confess."

"What is it you wear around your neck?"

Rising now Torquemada pushed back his chair and strode around the table to Alvero. They stood face to face and Alvero asked him in a whisper, "Why? Why, Thomas? Why are you doing this to me? What devil drives you?"

Torquemada reached out, grabbed the chain that was around Alvero's neck and lifted it over his head. "Still you wear it," Torquemada said. "Nothing can change you and no danger can teach you the meaning of fear."

"As I wear my honor."

"Honor?" Torquemada repeated, raising a brow and holding the ampule up before him.

"I care nothing for that," Alvero said fiercely. "That thing you hold in your fingers means nothing and it never meant anything. It is a memory, that's all it ever was, a meaningful memory. It was my father's and before him it belonged to his father and so when I kept it I had a memory of both of them. But in the nightmare that you and your kind have made of Spain, it becomes more than a memory. In this madness with which you hunt down anyone who has a spoonful of Jewish blood in his veins—it becomes a matter of pride. Shall I repeat that word for you, Torquemada? Pride! There is a Spanish word for you, Thomas. A good Spanish word. Do you know, my dear Thomas, I am a Christian but I am also a man and a Spaniard. If I threw away that thing that you are holding in your hand I might remain a Christian but I would cease to be a man and I would become the kind of Spaniard that Spain has sufficient of."

"You doom yourself," Torquemada said sadly.

"Goddamn you to hell!" Alvero shouted. "I was doomed the day the King of Spain asked you to taste my blood and share my wealth!"

CHAPTER TEN

AFTERWARDS the thing that Alvero remembered most about the torture chamber of the Inquisition was that time ceased. He was taken there first on the day before Holy Week began. The first time he was there they did little to him that was of any importance in terms of what became his existence—the method and meaning of torture. They pricked his skin with needles and they burned the flesh on his back with a hot iron, but it was enough to distort his time sense, and after that he had no idea nor was he ever able truly to recollect how many additional times they took him to torture.

He remembered things but he did not really remember the pain. Out of one time he remembered Thomas' face, cowled, expressionless, lit by a moving flame that passed back and forth like the pendulum of a clock. All the time that he, Alvero, stared at Thomas' face someone was screaming. It came as an afterthought to Alvero that he himself had been screaming, and that what he heard was the sound of his own screams.

Another time, all the while they were torturing him his gaze was fixed on an image of Christ on the cross which hung upon one wall of the torture room. This was a Gothic Christ, very lean, very realistic, red blood pouring from a wound in the image's side.

When he remembered, it always seemed to him that the image moved, tilted crazily and finally crashed upon the floor, but he knew that this was hallucination.

Most of his memory was of the ceiling of the Inquisition torture room. The ceiling was stone, and it was always wet and on its wet surface some sort of mold grew. Alvero remembered the ceiling very clearly from the time they had him on the rack. He would be looking at the ceiling and screaming with pain, when suddenly his vision would be blurred by the masked face of one of the torturers. That was the total symbol of the room. They were all masked with a black hood that had two eye holes and a third hole for breathing.

Another memory was of a single masked man. In Alvero's memory he was naked from head to foot, although in actuality he wore an apron of sorts over his nakedness. He was very heavily muscled and so strong that he often substituted his fingers for the instruments of torture. Even though he wore a mask Alvero always remembered him laughing with pleasure.

There was a time when they whipped Alvero and

all through that time in his memory there was the sound of church bells. After they whipped him they left him for long enough for his back to heal. That was the last of the torture. He remembered that one day while his back was still healing he managed to lift himself from his prison cot and go to the window —a tiny window high up in his prison cell—and to look out of it. That brought his eyes into a position a few inches above the ground level. Not far from where he was, a very young child played. This was a naked little boy of two years—one of the orphans who had been given shelter in the monastery. The little naked child played with a pigeon. The pigeon was without fear, and apparently he knew the child very well. He hopped over to the child and fluttered up onto the child's head, while the little boy giggled with delight.

Once during this period of torture, Alvero recalled to himself the letter he had written to Catherine. Strangely he remembered every word of the letter and he repeated aloud what he had written to her,

"You will remember my dear Catherine that once you said to me that of all the knights in Spain I was the finest. That was your judgment just as in my judgment you are the purest and the most beautiful of women. So I take this opportunity to remind you that even a knight bereft of all his weapons is defenseless. I sometimes feel that this is the way I stand at this moment. Defenseless and naked too. As I came into this world, so do I go out of it with all that I own surrendered to the King and the Inquisition. This has not yet happened but it will happen and nothing can stop it. Had I a son I would have managed at least to leave him my sword so that he might have with him always the knowledge that his father was a Spanish knight. But to you, my daughter, I can leave only a memory and that is a thing both precious and dangerous—"

He stopped remembering. It had become too painful.

The days passed and his back healed. There was no more torture. Twice a day bread, water and onions would be left in his cell. This was his diet and finally one day he slept and he awakened and there facing him at the foot of his bed was Torquemada. At first Alvero thought it was a hallucination, an illusion. During the time of his torture hallucinations had become a common occurrence in his life, and so he closed his eyes and waited a little while and then opened them again. Torquemada was still there.

Alvero reached out for the jug of water that stood on a table next to his bed. Torquemada handed this to him. Alvero drank and then sat up.

"Is there much pain, Alvero?" Torquemada asked.

"You ask me?"

"I ask you, Alvero—yes."

"What shall I tell you about pain, Thomas, my Father?" Alvero asked incredulously. "Shall I tell you what Christ felt when he was nailed onto the cross? I know."

"I also know."

"Do you, Thomas?"

Torquemada nodded. "God in heaven, what do you

think, Alvero? Do I love suffering? Am I a monster who feeds on death and misery?"

"Tell me—are you?"

Almost shrilly Torquemada cried, "I serve God!"

"I know." Alvero nodded. He filled his mouth with the rancid water from the jug, swallowed slowly. "You must forgive me, Thomas, because it is not easy for me to talk now, but as I said, I know. I have become a part of your devotion, Thomas. I know how you serve God. Oh how truly I know how you serve God!"

"I pleaded with you before, Alvero. I beg you now confess yourself and cut me down from my own cross."

"No!" Alvero shouted fiercely.

"You are without remorse and you are without pity."

"For you, Thomas? Pity for you? Is that what you are asking me to do—to pity you? Perhaps to pray for your salvation? Is that it?"

"God help me, do you think I have no love for you?"

"Love? No, Thomas—you put love away too long ago and you have no love for anything on this earth."

"I don't want you to die without grace or hope! I plead with you again," Torquemada said desperately.

Alvero smiled bitterly. "So you plead with me, Thomas."

Torquemada breathed deeply and then nodded. "As you will, Alvero." He sighed and turned toward the door. Alvero's voice stopped him.

"Thomas!"

Slowly Torquemada turned to Alvero. Alvero was amazed at the fact that the Prior's face was lit with hope.

"When must I die?" Alvero asked him.

"Soon, and may God have mercy upon you."

"Do you have mercy?"

"I cannot change it or stop it, Alvero. You know that. Don't think of what I would do or what I would not do. There is nothing that I can do."

"Do you have mercy?" Alvero repeated.

"What do you want, Alvero?"

"You know, don't you?"

"Perhaps."

"Send me the Rabbi Mendoza."

"So that both of us may be damned? Is that it, Alvero?"

"Send him to me," Alvero said softly. "As you value your own immortal soul, Torquemada, send him to me."

CHAPTER ELEVEN

I<small>N SEGOVIA</small> at that time there was a
plaza called *El Plaza de Fé* which meant that it was
the place of the *Auto de Fé*. The *Auto de Fé* is the
act of faith and the act of faith is the burning alive of
a human being for heresy. Even so long ago in Segovia people had forgotten who performs the act of
faith, he who is burned or he who does the burning.
In any case this plaza on the edge of the city aroused
mixed feelings in all who passed by it; and there
were times after an act of faith had been performed
when the stench of burning flesh lay about it so aw-
fully that only those with the strongest stomachs
could venture into the place.

On this night however when Torquemada walked
past the place of the act of faith and paused there for
a little while, the air was sweet and clean. There
had been no burning for heresy in eleven days. The
raised platform of stone, which was called the

pedestal of faith was swept clean and around the heavy, fire-blackened stake that rose out of it there were no ominous bundles of faggots. Instead a monk stood upon the stone platform with a scroll of parchment in his hands. Behind him stood a soldier of the Inquisition holding a pitch torch and giving him light to read. About thirty or forty people had gathered around to listen. For the most part, as Torquemada observed, they were beggars and sweepers, prostitutes and cutpurses—and among them, in and out of their legs, a dozen ragged, half-naked children ran and shouted and played.

As the monk began to read, Torquemada paused to listen. He stood on the edge of the crowd, half hidden in the shadows.

"These are the signatures of the devil," the monk read from the parchment scroll he held. His voice resonant and confident he cried out, "Open your eyes lest the sin be upon you, and by this shall ye know the Christian who is a Jew at heart, a Jew in secret, a Jew by night and in the darkness. By these things he will be recognized. Now heed me well. First of all if he celebrates the Sabbath, if he wears a clean shirt or better garments, if he spreads a clean cloth upon his table or lights no fire during that day or rests on that day, you will know him, and as God knows you so will you denounce him and call down the fires of wrath upon him—"

With the last of this the monk's voice rose to a high pitch. The crowd joined in screaming, hooting and clapping their hands. "God be praised!" someone in the crowd shouted. Others joined in. The children cupped their hands about their mouths and screamed with delight.

Finally the monk gave his parchment to the soldier to hold and spread his arms for silence. When it came he read from the parchment again,

"And by this too you will recognize him—if he eats meat during Lent, if he takes neither meat nor drink on the Day of Atonement—if he celebrates the Passover—" Now the monk interpolated. "Ah now there is opportunity for you. Always on the Passover the opportunity is greater. On the day of the Passover you watch him, you follow him, you notice him. Tempt him, offer him bread and see whether he puts the bread in his mouth. See whether he will touch the bread. Press the bread into his hand and see whether he drops it the way you would drop a hot coal. That way, cunningly, you will trap him and clothe your own immortal souls in specific grace—"

Torquemada walked away with long steps. He shivered a little and tried to throw off the great despondency that was gathering about him. He walked through street after street in Segovia, looking for a place he thought he remembered, and when he could not find it he called out to a boy. The child turned to run away, and Torquemada's voice lashed at him and caught him like a noose of cord,

"Boy—come here!" Trapped, enmeshed, the boy hesitated. Then he walked slowly to the grim towering figure of the Prior and stood in front of him waiting and silent.

"Boy, where is the house of the Rabbi Mendoza?" Torquemada asked.

The boy shook his head silently.

"Do you know who I am, boy?"

Still silent the boy nodded.

"Then do as I say and take me to the house."

Now the boy walked in front of Torquemada. The Prior followed and presently they came to a doorway in a wall, at which the boy pointed. Then the boy fled and Torquemada rapped sharply upon the door. He stood there waiting. A long time seemed to pass, so long that Torquemada began to wonder whether or not the boy had led him to an empty house. Then the door opened slowly, and a middle-aged woman stood in the doorway—a small plain-looking woman who regarded Torquemada without alarm but also without welcome.

"Who are you?" she asked.

"I am Prior Thomas de Torquemada."

"I know the name," the woman said, nodding slowly. "What do you want here, Prior?"

"To speak with the rabbi."

"We are Jews, Prior. Not Maranos—not converts or apostates or heretics. Only Jews. You have no business with us. Your Inquisition has no jurisdiction over Jews."

"Will you teach me the Law of the Church?" Torquemada demanded in sudden anger; and then catching himself, said more gently, "Still, I must talk with the rabbi."

For a moment longer the woman hesitated, observing Torquemada thoughtfully. Then she opened the door wide and stood aside, and Torquemada entered. She closed the door behind him. The hallway in which Torquemada stood was lit only by the light from the next room. In the pervasive darkness Torquemada stood and waited. "Follow me, please," Señora Mendoza said to him. She led him then into a plain room, which was about nine by fourteen feet. There was a small hearth at one side, a tile floor, plaster walls and windows on the inside wall which, Torquemada knew, would overlook whatever tiny courtyard they possessed. The furnishings consisted of a table, some chairs and a cupboard.

The table was set for supper for the rabbi and his wife. There were two plates, a bread, some cheese and olives and onions; and as Torquemada entered the room, the rabbi who was seated at the far end of the table rose and faced him. Silently the rabbi waited, until Torquemada asked impatiently,

"Don't you recognize me, Rabbi Mendoza?" Torquemada threw back his cowl.

"I know you, Prior," Mendoza said.

"As you know Don Alvero de Rafel."

To this Mendoza made no response by any sign or gesture. He simply stood at the end of the table, watching Torquemada.

"I say that you know him," Torquemada insisted.

Now Mendoza pushed the chair away and walked around the table to face the Prior. "Why do you confront me with these things?" he asked Torquemada, his voice almost desperate in its enticement of reason. "If I say that I know him—what then? You will send your soldiers to seize him. You will bring him to what you call a trial in the room of the Inquisition. You will accuse him and he will deny

145

the accusations. Then you will take him into that hellhole which you call the *room of faith* and you will torture him until his mind and his spirit break—"

Flatly and without apparent emotion Torquemada replied, "All that has been done, Rabbi. Now he lies in a cell of the Inquisition."

Shaking her head, Señora Mendoza sat down in a chair. The rabbi closed his eyes for a moment, his face full of pain. Then he controlled himself and asked softly and carefully, "What are you, Prior Torquemada? Our sages say that we are put upon this earth to comport ourselves in terms of our fellow man. All my life I have tried to understand men like you. Where even the cruelest or the dullest peon feeds on meat and bread, you feast on suffering."

"Feast? Oh no, Rabbi. There is no feast when you feel every twinge of pain in yourself."

"Do you, sir?" Mendoza asked. "And when you stand face to face with the Almighty, will you dare to explain the torture and death you have inflicted on so many by claiming that you felt their pain? Is this the sophistry that you render your God? Really, Prior, this kind of thinking is less than worthy of you. What do you know of pain, Prior?"

"I serve my God as he commands me, and I did not come here to argue theology with a Jew."

"Then why did you come here?"

"Because Alvero de Rafel pleaded with me to bring you to him—"

"And out of human kindness you agreed? Is that what you are trying to tell me? Am I a child? Am I a fool? Do you expect me to believe this incredible nonsense?"

"Are you God that I must explain myself?" Torquemada exclaimed. "For twenty years Alvero de Rafel was my friend."

"And out of the love you bore him, you arrested him and put him on the rack of torture—and presently you will tie him to that cursed stake in your place of faith and as further proof of the love in which you hold him, you will burn him and smell the stink of his burning flesh—"

"For his soul's salvation!" Torquemada cried.

Mendoza shook his head, turned away and walked across the room to where his wife sat. He put his hand upon her shoulder, sighed and said to Torquemada, "The thing we do most poorly is to hate. God help me, I pity you, Prior. All right, take me to him."

Now suddenly his wife rose and placed herself in front of him. "No!" she said. "No! I don't want you to go with him!"

"Don Alvero asked for me and I must go to him," Rabbi Mendoza explained.

"Not to the Inquisition," his wife begged. She turned to Torquemada, pointing a trembling hand at him. "Look at him. You know who he is and what he is."

"No, my dear," Mendoza told her patiently. "I don't know who he is or what he is. If only I knew that, I would have some peace. Even in this hellish nightmare-time that has fallen upon Spain I would have some peace. But I don't know who he is. I don't know what he is. May God forgive me, I don't know why he is. Nevertheless I must go with him."

The rabbi put his wife aside gently and went to the door. Torquemada followed him.

They walked together through the streets of the town, side by side. A moon was rising and there was light enough for them to see their way. For a time they walked in silence and then Mendoza asked Torquemada whether or not he felt fear when he walked alone in the night with a rabbi and a Jew. The question contained a note of sad mockery. Yet Torquemada took the words upon their face value and replied firmly,

"I fear only God."

"Yet people see us," Mendoza continued. "Even in the darkness they will recognize you and they will recognize me. Suppose one of them should whisper to another—Torquemada Judaizes? Suppose the whisper took wings as whispers do—"

"Only the devil would say that," Torquemada replied.

Mendoza nodded. "Yes, the devil. What a burden he bears! And tell me this, Prior. If one should remember that only a century ago there was a good and pious rabbi in Barcelona whose name was Torquemada? The devil remembers everything, does he not, Prior?"

"You dare too much, Jew!" Torquemada said angrily.

"We all dare too much, Prior," Mendoza agreed. "It is the penalty for existence. However, we Jews do not put the same trust in the act of confession

148

that you do. Therefore I do not ask you to confess yourself."

"Ask me nothing, Jew! And keep quiet! I have no need of your talk."

"As you will." Mendoza shrugged. "My talk is witless and far from entertaining, and as for Torquemada, well, let me tell you, Prior, there are a thousand men in Spain who have that name. It is a very common name. So you see that my cunning is rather childlike and entirely wasted."

CHAPTER TWELVE

THROUGH HIS SLEEP, his dreams, his nightmares and his twisted pain-filled memories, Alvero heard Torquemada's voice. He saw Torquemada's face. His mouth burned with thirst and Torquemada held a glass of cool wine in front of him, smiling. Then the face disappeared and there was only the voice. Dry, nasal, imperious, it issued its commands. Alvero heard the voice say,

"Give me the key and the torch. You can find your way to the door in the dark."

Alvero opened his eyes. Through the tiny window in the door to his cell there was a flickering flow of torchlight. Torquemada's voice again, "Yes this is his cell."

A key turned in the door and it ground open. The torch entered. Alvero sat up in bed rubbing his eyes and then he saw that Torquemada stood in his cell holding a flaming pitch torch and that another

man stood next to Torquemada. The light of the
torch was almost blinding and at first Alvero could
not face it. He closed his eyes and then opened
them to slits. He rubbed them, opened them wider
and forced himself to look at the dancing light of the
torch. It seemed to him then that the man with
Torquemada was the Rabbi Benjamin Mendoza, but
of this Alvero was not sure—just as he was not sure
that what he was seeing was not an illusion or a
dream.

Then the apparition that appeared to be Mendoza
spoke to him and asked him whether he was in pain.
Alvero managed to get to his feet and to cover the
two steps that separated him from Mendoza. He
touched Mendoza and convinced himself that Mendoza was real. Then he touched Torquemada. Torquemada did not move, only standing there with the
hissing, burning torch, and then Alvero reached up
and pushed away Torquemada's cowl so that he
could see the man's face.

Torquemada nodded to him. "So it is, Don Alvero," Torquemada said.

Then Alvero turned away and sat down once
more on his bed. He looked at the rabbi for a while
before he answered him. "Pain? There is pain. But
I am learning to live with pain, and I think I am
learning to die with pain. I thank you for coming
here."

The rabbi nodded and Alvero asked Torquemada
whether he would leave the two of them alone.

Torquemada shook his head. "I jeopardize my
soul enough by bringing the Jew to you."

"Then take him away," Alvero said petulantly. "Take him away before he says anything. Whatever he says will be evidence given against himself. Then you will accuse him."

"I will not accuse him," Torquemada said.

"I don't believe you!" Alvero spat the words out with contempt.

"I give you my word!" Torquemada cried.

"Believe him," Mendoza told Alvero. "Believe him, my son. He gives you his word. Do not question his word."

"Do you believe him?" Alvero asked.

"I believe him—yes, I do," Mendoza replied.

With this Alvero leaned back against the wall for a long moment closing his eyes. When he opened them again the two men still stood there. Alvero felt very tired. "Rabbi," he said hopelessly, "will you tell me something?"

"Yes, my son?"

"Am I Christian or Jew?"

"Christian, my son."

"The Inquisition," Alvero said painfully, the act of speech becoming increasingly difficult, "accused me of the heresy of Judaizing. I wore an ampule on the chain around my neck. I wore it with a cross. The ampule and the cross lay side by side upon my breast. It was my father's. Inside it on a bit of parchment were the words: And thou shalt love the Lord thy God with all thy heart and all thy soul and all thy might. Do you know what this is, Rabbi?"

"I know."

"Is it a curse?" Alvero asked.

"No, it is not a curse."

"I am a Christian," Alvero said, "yet I must die for this thing, for this cursed idiocy I must die—I wore that ampule around my neck."

"Why did you wear it, Don Alvero?"

"I don't know," Alvero said.

"Yet you knew the danger?"

"I knew the danger," Alvero agreed, looking at Torquemada. Torquemada avoided his gaze, stared straight ahead of him, a carven black figure holding a burning and sizzling torch.

"Did you want to be a Jew?" Mendoza asked.

"I don't know. The notion never occurred to me. I never said to myself, Alvero de Rafel, do you want to be a Jew or a Christian or a Muslim. Why should I say such a thing to myself? I was a Christian knight of Spain. I had all that a man could desire for happiness. Tell me, why should I desire to be a Jew?"

"I cannot answer that, Don Alvero."

"No, I don't suppose you can," Alvero agreed, "but the man who felt that way, Rabbi Mendoza, no longer exists. What exists sits before you in this cell. Look at me. Look at me—because now I say to you, Rabbi, make me a Jew!"

Without moving, Torquemada said violently, "No!"

The rabbi turned to Torquemada and said quietly, "Peace, Prior. Can I make him a Jew?"

"You can and you must!" Alvero insisted.

"Why?" Torquemada asked Alvero. "Why?"

"So that what you are and what I am will be set apart forever!"

"To burn in hell for all eternity?" Torquemada demanded.

"Yes! Joyfully! Gladly!" Alvero cried fiercely.

"Don Alvero," Mendoza said, shaking his head. "Is it as simple as that? If God chose the Jews—and one can't imagine why except to suffer so that we bear for eternity what the man, your Savior, bore for a few hours on the cross—if this is truly the case it does not hold within it an invitation. We happen to be Jews—in a mystery that preoccupies us beyond solution. I cannot make you a Jew—"

Alvero rose to his feet and standing there unsteadily pleaded his case, held out one hand to the rabbi and insisted, "But you can! You must!"

"Listen to me, now," Mendoza said. "Please, may I beg you, listen to me. There was a Jewish sage of blessed memory who was called the Rabbi Hillel, and to him there came a heathen who said, 'Rabbi, make me a Jew.' Rabbi Hillel answered, 'I cannot make you a Jew, for only he is a Jew who knows the Law and follows it.' Then, with great distress, the heathen answered, 'How can I know the Law when men study it for a whole lifetime and even then do not know it?' To which the Rabbi Hillel then replied, 'Truly, to know the Law a lifetime is little enough, but that is in one manner of speaking. I can teach the Law to you in a single sentence. This then is the Law,' said the Rabbi Hillel, 'to love thy brother as thyself. That is the whole of the Law, and all the rest is commentary.' So said the most blessed of all our sages." The rabbi paused now, and it seemed to Alvero that he was attempting to recapture what he had just said, to contemplate it and to use it in some way—and it also seemed to Alvero that in this he failed as he said, "Do you understand me, Don Alvero?"

"No more than you understand me," Alvero whispered.

"I understand you," the rabbi said.

"Then in the name of God—your God or my God, do what I ask!"

"Out of hatred for him?" Mendoza inquired, pointing to Torquemada.

"Shall I love him?" Alvero demanded. He too pointed to Torquemada now. "Look at him! Only look at him! The anointed!" The effort left Alvero exhausted. Trembling, he sank back onto his bed.

"There is no more to do here," Torquemada said to Mendoza. "Let us go."

"Don Alvero," Mendoza said, "listen to me. Think about what I said to you. If you came to me and said, 'Make me a man,' then what could I say to you? What you are, God made you, and you are no more and no less—"

"You talk in riddles," Alvero muttered hopelessly.

"As we all do," Mendoza admitted.

"Enough," Torquemada said. He walked through the door and waited for Mendoza. When Mendoza had left the cell, Torquemada closed the door and turned the key in the lock.

CHAPTER THIRTEEN

AFTER TORQUEMADA HAD LEFT the Place of the Act of Faith, the monk had continued his reading of the proclamation for the recognition of Judaizers. However, the proclamation was very long, and as the monk continued to intone the endless signs and symbols by which one could recognize Jews, the crowd began to disperse. First the children lost interest and went home to whatever suppers awaited them and to whatever piles of rags constituted their beds. Then the prostitutes drifted away because this was the beginning of their working day, the hour when the first customers would come to seek them out. Then, one by one, the thieves, the pursesnatchers, the loafers and the cutthroats departed.

Only a single person remained as the monk finished reading, rolled up his parchment, delivered his blessing and then walked away into the darkness with the soldier of the Inquisition. This single small person left at the edge of the stone platform was wrapped from head to foot in a dark cloak. She sat upon a low stone with her back against the platform. Perhaps an hour passed and still she sat there and then a voice cried out,

"Catherine! Are you here? Catherine! Is it you?"

Juan Pomas came into the Place of the Act of Faith. The moon was rising now and there was enough light for him to see the small figure huddled at the edge of the platform.

"Is it you, Catherine?"

The cloaked figure rose and stood waiting. Juan Pomas strode over to her and then she opened her cloak and uncovered her head.

"My God, Catherine," Juan said. "My God—you made me sick with fear—looking everywhere for you. It is late at night. Don't you realize that? You can't stay here alone. This is no place to be alone. It swarms with cutthroats and thieves."

"Where shall I go, Juan?" she asked simply.

"I'll take you home."

"Home? Whose home will you take me to? Where is a home that will open its doors to me?"

"Your own home," Juan answered impatiently.

"I have no home."

"You make no sense when you talk like that, Catherine. What do you mean you have no home? You don't know how troubled your mother is. She is sick with fear—so sick with it that she had to take to her bed."

"Are you troubled, Juan?"

"Of course I am."

"Did you betray him?"

"Catherine, what has come over you? I don't know you anymore. Sometimes you say things that I don't understand at all. I don't know what you're saying now."

"You know what I am saying." Catherine nodded. "I am asking a very simple question. Did you betray him, Juan?"

Juan stared at her without replying. He swallowed, opened his mouth to speak, allowed the words to die unspoken and looked at her again.

"Go away from me," Catherine said in disgust.

Instead he moved toward her. He reached out his hand to her arm and she shook it off, leaping back away from him. He came toward her and she stepped onto the rock where she had been sitting and from there onto the platform, crouching there and crying out at him,

"No! Don't touch me!"

"You'll wake all of Segovia shouting like that," Juan said hoarsely.

"Just go away from here," she said. "That's all, go away."

For a minute or so more he stood there, and then he turned around and walked off into the darkness. Catherine collapsed onto the stones of the platform. They were still warm from the sun. She curled up there on the stones, her cloak over her. She must have slept for a while. When she opened her eyes it was still night. There was no sound in the Place of the Act of Faith. The night was cool and she shivered under her cloak. She dropped off again, and a ghastly dream awakened her. In the dream she saw her father on the rack in the torture chamber of the Inquisition. He was screaming and pleading for her to release him from his pain. She woke up weeping. Dawn had come, the first pink color of the sun over the rooftops of Segovia. The place of faith was empty, silent and abandoned.

Catherine climbed down from the platform and walked into the streets of Segovia until she came to a common fountain. She felt terribly dry and when she reached the fountain she drank and drank. However, she was not hungry. She continued to walk then through Segovia in the opposite direction from her home.

The city was waking, cocks crowed, chickens and goats were released from their pens. Children were turned out to play. The smoke of morning fires rose over the town and the pungent smell of charcoal burning filled the air.

Now Catherine walked through the Jewish quarter. From the houses here the men were emerging and going to worship. Catherine had been in the Jewish quarter before, but only to pass through it on a horse or in a litter. She had never walked in it on foot, close to the life it contained and to some measure partaking of that life.

She was not afraid of the Jews—but neither did she feel that she was a part of them. They were more often bearded than the Christian Spaniards and more heavily bearded. They moved quickly and purposefully. Only Catherine was without purpose as she followed them, and presently she came to their destination, the synagogue.

She had never been inside a synagogue before nor had she any clear purpose in entering one now. She did not say to herself, "I will go into the synagogue." Neither did she say to herself, "No, I don't want to go into the synagogue." It was a thing she neither wanted nor avoided—and yet she went in. The synagogue was there and she entered it. If someone had asked her whether she had to enter it she would only have shrugged her shoulders. There were no hard and definite decisions within her.

She was the last person to enter the synagogue, and then the beadle, a tiny man with a snow-white beard, closed the door behind her. Inside the synagogue now there were about forty men but no other woman than Catherine.

She looked around her now, and she had the sense of a building that was very ancient. Unlike a church, its interior was perfectly rectangular. On each side, as she entered, there was a very low balcony. Catherine realized that this area must have been reserved for the women, since the men sat in the lower space. She had heard that men and women sat apart in the synagogue. The women's sections were raised about a foot higher than the central part of the synagogue. They were separated from the central part by solid wooden railings and the railings were joined to the ceiling by a series of posts.

In the women's part of the synagogue the benches —the only seating accommodations were plain, bare benches—ran parallel with the length of the hall. In the men's area the benches were set parallel with the width of the hall. At the front of the synagogue, that is, the part opposite the door, there was a plain pulpit and behind the pulpit an area covered with a crimson drape. The pulpit was raised two steps from the floor, and on the pulpit there was a wooden lectern with an open parchment scroll upon it.

Catherine took her place in one of the side sections. On the pulpit there was a man whom Catherine recognized as the rabbi who had come to their house—the rabbi whose life her father had saved. He took hold of the scroll by its handles and moved it, turning both ends until he came to that section which he sought. Then he saw Catherine sitting alone at the other end of the synagogue. He met her gaze, and it seemed to Catherine that he paused to consider and to examine himself as well as the scroll in front of him. He stood thus for a substantial length of time without opening his mouth, without speaking or moving, and then he turned to the scroll and began to read,

"My God, my God—why have you forsaken me? Why so far from helping me? From the sound of my pleading? Oh my God, I cry out in the daytime but you hear me not. And in the nighttime I cry out. I am not silent—" He paused then, laid his hand flatly upon the open scroll and looked at Catherine. Then he looked around at the various faces in the congregation and said to them,

"Forgive me if I speak with a different voice and make a different prayer on this strange morning.

166

Someone has come among us. I was called upon to make a decision but I can make no decision. So I read what my fathers have written—"

Even as Mendoza was speaking threads of smoke trickled under the door and into the synagogue, filling the old building with harsh smell and crackling noise. The old beadle ran to the door of the synagogue and tried to open it. It opened outward, but now it would not respond to his efforts.

"Help me! Help me!" he cried. Men from the congregation rushed to help him. Catherine sat unmoving. Mendoza, pitching his voice high, read,

"Holy is the Lord. All the praises of Israel make a tent for you. Our fathers trusted in you. They trusted and you delivered them from evil. They cried out to you and you heard them and they were delivered. They trusted in you and their trust was not confounded—"

The crackling sound had become a roar now. Strangely as if the information of her own senses was coming from a great distance, Catherine realized that men outside were burning the synagogue. The people in the synagogue were trapped there. The whole Jewish quarter had become a Place of the Act of Faith, and in the midst of it the old building burned like tinder.

CHAPTER FOURTEEN

THE ROOM in which Torquemada lived his life at this time was not much larger than the cell in which Alvero lay. The room had a floor of black tile and walls of white plaster. Its only ornamentation—if one can consider it such—was a crucifix which hung from one wall. In addition to this there was a chair in the room and a bed and a small chest of drawers. In front of the crucifix there was a hempen mat and it was on this mat that Torquemada was kneeling when a monk knocked at his door.

"Come in," Torquemada said.

The monk entered. Torquemada remained where he was, unmoving. The only illumination in the room was a bar of light that fell upon Torquemada from a high window in the wall of the cell. The monk stood inside the door and waited. Finally Torquemada finished with his devotions and rose and turned to face the monk, the broad band of light falling between them.

"Well, Brother?" Torquemada asked.

"They burned the synagogue," the monk replied.

Torquemada's face tightened and he nodded. "I saw the smoke. I smelled the smoke. Who burned the synagogue, Brother?"

"People—good people—"

"Good people? Or thieves and cutthroats?"

"Good Christians," the monk said defensively.

"Good Christians." Torquemada nodded. "Were there people in the synagogue when it burned? Were the Jews at their prayers?"

"It was the time of their prayers," the monk said.

"Were any saved?"

"No. They all died. The wood was very old. You know how old the wood was, Prior. You know how old the synagogue was."

"I know." Torquemada nodded.

"As old as time," the monk went on, "I have heard it said that the devil built the building before there were any human beings in Spain and then he gave it to the Jews—"

"Don't talk like a fool!" Torquemada interrupted him. "Did the whole building burn?"

"It went up like a torch."

"Who was there?"

"About forty Jews," the monk said, "and the Rabbi Mendoza."

"No others?"

"And a woman."

"A woman?" Torquemada came close to the monk

now so that their faces were only inches apart. "What do you mean—a woman? Few of the Jewish women go to the synagogue—except on the Sabbath."

"This was not a Jewish woman," the monk said defensively.

"How do you know?" Torquemada demanded.

"By the way she was dressed. She wore the clothes of a Spanish lady of wealth. She was covered with a cloak but when it fell away from her I saw the jewels she wore."

"Did you recognize her?"

"I am not sure, Prior." The monk was defensive, almost pleading. He wanted to move in a safe direction but he could not for the life of him anticipate what direction Torquemada desired him to move in. "She was a Christian woman," he insisted.

"Old? Young? Of middle years? Think, you fool! What was she like? What was her appearance?"

"She was very young, I think. She put me in mind of the daughter of Don Alvero."

"Why didn't you stop her?" Torquemada cried, his voice shrill and fierce.

The monk cowered away from him, demanding, "Was it my place to stop her, Prior? She was a heretic the moment she set foot in there. Tell me—how is it my duty to stop her? It was only my duty to watch her and denounce her. God himself consumed her."

Suddenly Torquemada grasped the monk's robe in his clenched fists, drew him close and whispered, "How dare you?"

"What have I done?" the monk begged, panic-stricken.

Torquemada let go of the man and thrust him away. "What have you done! Do penance until you know what you have done. A hundred days on bread and water will sharpen your knowledge of sin! A hundred nights naked on your bed will sharpen your sodden sensitivity!"

The monk dropped to his knees now, stammering, "Please—please, Prior—how have I sinned? Tell me how I have sinned."

"Get out of here!" Torquemada roared. "Leave me!"

The monk climbed to his feet and fled from the room. Torquemada stood there alone, his eyes closed, his fists clenched and finally he whispered, "God—pity me—"

CHAPTER FIFTEEN

AFTER THE MONK HAD LEFT, Torquemada sat for almost an hour in the darkness of his room. The fires of hell closed in upon him but he endured—and he did not question God or God's reasons. Once, aloud, he said,

"I am your instrument."

This did not comfort Torquemada. It was simply an acknowledgment of himself to himself. At last he rose and went out of the room and walked through the corridors of the priory. There was no one in the priory who had the courage to face him in his anger and the word had gone about that he was filled with anger. The passageways were deserted. He went down the wet stone stairs to the place where the Inquisition cells were and he came into the circle of radiance cast by a pitch torch. Taking this torch from its bracket he continued along the passageway until he came to Alvero's cell. He opened the door and went in. Alvero lay on his bed asleep.

Torquemada stood over Alvero watching him as

he slept. Alvero slept peacefully, breathing long and deeply; his sleep was innocent and untroubled. Torquemada felt a fierce wave of envy, and an even fiercer sense of hatred, but this hatred came and went; and suddenly Alvero opened his eyes and sat up, covering his eyes at first from the glare of the torch and then opening them wide to see Torquemada.

"I had no dreams," Alvero said. "The dreams are here. Have you ever thought, Thomas, that with all our tales of hell we may be closer to the truth of it than we ever imagine? Have you ever thought that perhaps this whole world of ours is simply the hell of another existence?"

"More blasphemy?" Torquemada asked woodenly.

"How many times will you kill me?" Alvero shrugged. "How many times will you burn me?"

Alvero stared at his hands for a moment or two and then he asked softly, "Is it time, Thomas?"

"Time for what?"

"For me to die."

"It is not time for you to die," Torquemada replied.

"Then why have you come? You intrude on me, Thomas. All I have left is the privilege of being alone with myself, but you stand in front of me like an accusing angel. Or is it an accusing devil? What do you want, Thomas? Are you here for my soul's sake? You have always been most profoundly concerned with the health of my immortal soul. Shall I confess myself, Thomas?"

"For my own soul's sake, I think," Torquemada replied.

Alvero found that amusing. He began to laugh. The laughter took hold of him and he found that his whole body was shaking with it. He could not stop himself. He doubled over with the laughter until Torquemada cried out,

"Stop it! Stop it!"

"Your soul's sake, Thomas! Thomas, Thomas, I never thought to live to see the day when you would doubt your soul—and undertake something for your soul's sake. Have you ever seen your soul, Thomas? Your soul is black, Thomas—black as pitch, but shrouded in gold. Festooned with a million pieces of gold all of them robbed from all the poor devils you burn in your Act of Faith. Thomas—Thomas, you are a bitter accusation against mankind. The Good Lord is an idiot—or he never would have let the waters of the flood recede. But why should I doubt you, Thomas? If you should ever step over the edge of eternity and plunge into the pit of hell all the angels will come singing to catch you, to rescue you and to welcome your stinking immortal soul. To heaven, I hope—believe me, Thomas, that is a most fervent hope. I pray that hope every night to three gods. The God of the Jews, the God of the Christians and the God of the Muslims; to all three of them. I pray that they will open their arms and welcome your stinking, shining soul to heaven. Do you know why? Can you think of a good reason why, Thomas?" Alvero waited, smiling up at Torquemada's face; and in spite of himself Torquemada was moved to ask,

"Why?"

"The answer is obvious"—Alvero smiled—"and

simple and direct—an assurance to me that if I spend
an eternity in hell I will never have to see your
face."

"You have courage, Alvero," Torquemada admitted.

"Courage!" Alvero cried, rising to his feet. "To hell
with courage! What is courage? When you reach the
end there is no more distance to go. If you fall off a
cliff there is no way back. I have nothing to lose,
Thomas. Will you burn me twice? Three times? Ten
times?"

"Not even once," Torquemada said tonelessly. "I
am going to release you."

Alvero went close to Torquemada now, face to
face, and whispered to him, "What is this, Thomas?
Have you had a bellyful of the rack and the thumb-
screws? Is this some new method of torture, more
refined, more delicate?"

"I am telling you the truth. I am going to release
you."

"No," Alvero said. "No, not at all." He turned back
to his bed and sat down, staring at the floor of his
cell, and he muttered, "No one has ever come alive
from the presence of Torquemada. I know you like a
book, Thomas—like a book of death. Death is the
only friend Torquemada has—death and the torture
room. How many hundreds have you condemned
to death, Thomas?"

"But you knew this," Torquemada reminded him.
"You knew this and you remained my friend. You
remained my friend because you were secure in my
faith—"

"I am paying my price!" Alvero interrupted him.

"Don't talk to me about your faith. We don't share a faith. We share nothing."

Torquemada nodded and said, almost with detachment and utterly without emotion, "Nevertheless you will be released, Alvero. All your possessions are subject to seizure and they become the property of the Holy Inquisition. I would counsel you to go away. Go empty-handed—for this is the way we come into the world, and for you, Alvero de Rafel, it is a departure as profound, I think, as the departure that comes with death. So I say to you, go away. Your possessions are forfeit but you may take a single horse and a saddle and sidearms. You will leave here, and you will do this tonight. If you are in Segovia tomorrow I shall issue orders for your arrest."

Staring unbelievingly at Torquemada, Alvero stood up again. Torquemada went to the door of the cell and swung it open and pointed and said,

"Go now, Alvero. I will light your way out and through the passage."

Alvero went to him, and as he walked he asked the Prior in a whisper, "Do you mean this? God help me, in all truth, Thomas, are you lying to me? Are you playing games with me? You were my friend once—understand that I can endure very little more—"

"I mean it!" Torquemada said savagely.

Alvero stared at him. "I cannot thank you—I will not thank you. God damn you, I would almost rather die than have a kindness from you! I will not owe my life to you!"

Torquemada walked through the door and Alvero followed him, followed the circle of radiance that meant life or death, truth or falsehood, all the world or no world whatsoever. Raging and doubting Alvero followed him, and Torquemada answered thoughtfully,

"There speaks the Spaniard, not the Jew. I do you no kindness. I repay a debt."

"What debt?" Alvero shouted. "You have no debts to me!"

"Don't keep trying me," Torquemada replied angrily, "and don't misjudge me, Alvero—for even as you hate me, I hate you!"

Alvero walked with Torquemada now, walked in the circle of light from the pitch torch, through the passageway, and in the course of his steps he nodded, clenched his fists and nodded again and agreed with the Prior.

"Best!" Alvero said. "That way is best, Thomas. With hate, Thomas. Always with hate. That way we will remember each other."

Torquemada made no answer to this, but led Alvero along the corridor and up the staircase and through the priory and into the cool of the afternoon. They waited and stood looking across the gardens, while in response to Torquemada's order a monk brought Alvero his horse. Alvero mounted. There was no farewell and no words between the two men.

Alvero rode away but he looked back once and saw Torquemada standing there in front of the cloister. Torquemada stood tall and grim and—it seemed to Alvero—his face was etched in pain. But when Alvero looked again there was only a man—a righteous and awful man.

CHAPTER SIXTEEN

ALVERO PEERED into the long gallery of his home. A fire was burning and Maria sat in a chair facing the flames. He did not enter but went to his room, where he looked at himself in a long mirror. The filthy, cadaverous and bearded stranger who returned his glance was not recognizable, even to Alvero. What was himself had disappeared, perhaps forever; and he had a feeling of emptiness, of utter despair—as if he were already dead and lost beyond finding, nor did this feeling go away when he had shaved off his beard, sponged the dirt from his body and dressed himself.

The house was strangely quiet. He had hoped at first that his daughter Catherine would not interrupt him until he was clean and clad in fresh clothes, but now he wondered where she was and why he heard no sound to indicate her presence. He was overtaken by a sudden anxiety and he finished dressing hurriedly. He dressed for the road, in leather trousers and a leather coat, and he drew on long, tough riding boots. He buckled on sword and dagger, and then in defiance of Torquemada's instructions dropped a dozen gold pieces into his boots. Whether he would come back to Segovia or leave Segovia tonight or wait until the next morning and leave then, he had not decided, but he knew that in Spain as elsewhere a man does not travel without money.

Dressed, armed and spurred, he strode into the gallery where his wife sat. She looked up at him as he entered but on her face there was no greeting, not even recognition. Dully and flatly she asked him,

"Why are you here?"

Alvero had expected the unexpected but not this, and almost pleadingly he demanded whether she had known where he was.

"I knew," Maria said.

"Look!" Alvero cried holding out his left hand with its broken nails and its smashed half-healed thumb.

Maria looked at it and said, "God's judgment."

"What the devil are you talking about!" Alvero exclaimed striding across the gallery and back. She turned her head away from him and he grasped her by the shoulder and swung her to him.

"Don't touch me."

"Is this my welcome?" Alvero shouted. "Is this how a man returns from the dead to his wife?"

"I am not your wife."

Alvero stared at her, shook his head and said

hopelessly, "Maria—what devil has taken hold of you?"

She answered woodenly, "I have not sinned, I have not transgressed. I will not be burned. I will not be tortured."

"Maria, Maria—it's all right. No one will harm you now. I'll tell you what I have decided. I have decided that we must all go away—all of us and together. We must never be separated." He waited for an answer and she stared at him without comprehension and still without recognition.

"Where is Catherine?" he said suddenly.

"Catherine—"

"Is she in her room?"

"She is dead. That was God's judgment too."

Alvero stood there. He heard the words and they echoed in his mind without meaning. He smiled—and then he realized that he was smiling foolishly. He almost began to laugh but then he went to Maria and grasped her arm so that she winced and whimpered with pain.

"Where is Catherine?" he shouted at the top of his voice.

"Jew! Let go of me!"

Maria stood up and managed to pull free of Alvero. She went around behind the chair, rubbing her bruised wrist and said slowly, emphasizing each word separately,

"I-cannot-stand-to-be-touched-by-a-Jew."

Alvero stared at her in horror and disbelief and at that moment Julio came into the room. When he saw Alvero he stopped and stared at Alvero as a man

stares at a ghost. Alvero ran toward him. Julio's first
response was to turn in flight, but Alvero caught
him and swung him around and demanded harshly,
wildly,

"Julio, where is Catherine?"

Julio did not answer this and Alvero shook him
angrily and cried out, "Damn your soul—damn you
to hell, answer me! Where is she?"

Then Julio looked at Alvero so woefully that Alvero let go of him. Julio's jaw dropped. He spoke
with effort, gasping for each word,

"She is dead, master."

"Dead? No, no you are lying!" Alvero nodded at
Julio. "Yes, you are lying, aren't you, Julio? Games,
or you are punishing me. I blasphemed, you are
punishing me. No, don't torture me. Just tell me,
Julio, it's a lie, isn't it?"

"Master, would to God that I was lying to you. But
I am telling you the truth. She went into the synagogue—"

"The synagogue?" Alvero interrupted. "No, no,
that must have been someone else, Julio. Why should
she go into the synagogue? There would be no reason, no reason for her to go into the synagogue."

"Yes, yes, master," Julio moaned. "The synagogue,
that's where she went, and then they burned it down.
I ran there. The whole town ran there but it was too
late. They burned it down."

"You saw her?" Alvero whispered.

"I brought her body back with me," Julio said. He
was weeping now.

"Where is her body?" Alvero asked. "Where did you put her?"

"In her room, master," Julio replied, "but don't go there. Don't go to her room. Don't look at her. I tell you, master, she was burned in a fire. Don't look at her. I covered over her body—"

Julio tried to stop Alvero, but Alvero flung him aside and walked through the door and up the stairs to his daughter's room. He went in there and something lay covered on the bed and Alvero uncovered it. After a while Alvero covered the body again and went down and back to the gallery.

Just outside of the door of the gallery he heard Juan Pomas' voice and then he heard Julio say,

"Señor Pomas—go away. Go away quickly."

"Doña Maria," Juan said to Alvero's wife, "tell me, is it true that Catherine is dead?"

No reply from Maria, but Julio's voice was high-pitched, shrill with fear as he pleaded with Juan, "Yes, Señor Pomas—she is dead—just as this house is dead. Now go away quickly—"

Alvero went to the door of the gallery then, and he saw Juan thrust Julio from him and demand to know how Julio dared to lay hands upon him.

"Not now," Julio pleaded. "This is not a time for pride, believe me, Señor Pomas. Don Alvero is here in this house with his daughter's body."

In sudden fear mixed with disbelief Juan shook his head and insisted that Alvero was with the Inquisition or dead.

"You cursed young fool!" Julio cried. "I tell you he is inside. If he finds you here—"

"And if he does?" Juan Pomas blustered.

"Don't you think he knows who betrayed him? Don't you think everyone knows?"

"How does he know?"

Alvero was in the room now. He walked toward Juan and Julio saw him, but Juan's back was to him. Maria saw him and screamed. In a voice as cold as ice Alvero said to Juan,

"Because a dog's bark sounds far!"

Now Juan turned to face him and Julio came between them, but Alvero pushed past him. Juan Pomas tore his dagger from his scabbard but Alvero seized the dagger wrist and twisted it so brutally that the dagger clattered to the floor. Pomas screamed with pain, and then both of Alvero's hands closed around his neck and he screamed no more.

"For my life nothing!" Alvero shouted. "No meaning or value! My life and your life, they are dirt! But for my daughter's life—" There was no passion now. Coldly and deliberately Alvero began to choke Juan to death. Juan struggled, tore at Alvero's hands, struck his face and then his struggles weakened and his arms dropped.

Maria stood up and walked toward them. Loudly and shrilly she cried out to her husband, "Jew, is this how you become a Jew—to murder a Spanish gentleman? Jew, let go of him! Jew! Filthy Jew!"

Alvero let go of Juan. The anger was gone. The hate was gone. He simply let go of Juan and Juan Pomas sank to the floor, choking, gasping, rubbing his throat and fighting for his breath. Then Alvero turned and stared at his wife. She met his gaze.

They looked at each other and then she turned and walked from the room. Alvero went to the table, pulled out his chair, sat down and leaned over the table panting. Juan Pomas watched him. Then Juan Pomas got up carefully and then he ran. As from a great distance Alvero listened to his running steps and then heard him mount his horse and then heard the wild headlong gallop of the horse as Juan Pomas fled.

Julio stood waiting and finally Alvero said to him, "Come, old friend. We have much to do." He climbed wearily upstairs to Catherine's room while Julio went for a shovel and pick. Alvero wrapped Catherine's body in a silken coverlet, lifted it in his arms and took it down to the garden. He and Julio took turns digging the grave. It was slow work. The little strength that remained to Alvero was draining from him, and Julio was an old man, but at last the grave was deep enough and Alvero and Julio eased the body into it and then filled the grave with dirt.

Alvero was trembling with the effort. "I need a drink," he said to Julio, "and a piece of bread. Can you saddle my horse?" Julio nodded and Alvero went into the house and poured himself a glass of wine and took some bread from the cupboard. The bread was tasteless in his mouth but he forced himself to eat it and to wash it down with the wine. What was left of the bread he put in one pocket of his riding jacket and he filled the other pocket with cold meat and cheese. Then he walked through the gallery. It was empty and the candles had burned out, but the light of dawn was in the sky already and he was able to see his way. When he came to the stables in back of the house Julio had the horse saddled. He held the horse for Alvero to mount and then hanging onto Alvero's stirrup he said to him brokenly,

"Master, take me with you."

"No, old friend. I ride faster than my memories and I ride alone. You have shared enough with me. The particular hell that waits for me is singular, only singular—"

"I will help you," Julio begged him. "I will look after you—take care of you—"

"Nothing can help me, Julio, and even God will not look after me. We do what we can, each of us. I bid you farewell." He spurred the horse then through the gate and out onto the road that ran north from Segovia.

Julio remained in front of the stable until the sound of hoofbeats had ceased. Then because even an old man must live Julio went into the house to satisfy his hunger.

G47